GONE WITH THE SIN
(BOOK 8)

A Harley & Davidson Mystery Series

LILIANA HART
SCOTT SILVERII

7th Press

We want to dedicate our eighth book in the series to our friends in Rusty Gun, Texas. We appreciate everyone who has joined us to share in Hank and Agatha's adventures.

Here's to you!

**Check Out The COMPLETE List Of Books &
Learn More About Your AUTHORS**

The Harley and Davidson Mystery Series
The Farmer's Slaughter
A Tisket a Casket
I Saw Mommy Killing Santa Claus
Get Your Murder Running
Deceased and Desist
Malice in Wonderland
Tequila Mockingbird
Gone With the Sin

Chapter One

TUESDAY

Agatha Harley loved Rusty Gun, Texas. She loved the quaint scenery and simple way of life, and she loved the quirks of the people who lived there. For the most part.

The Kettle Café was jam-packed with the early morning breakfast crowd, and Agatha and her best friend, Heather Cartwright, were in their usual booth having breakfast. They tried to get together once a week to stay caught up on the goings-on in Rusty Gun, but since Heather's unfortunate run-in with the law after her ex-husband's murder, she'd spent the last several months traveling and flitting back to town whenever she started to miss her current boy toy too much.

Breakfast had been going well until The Daughters of the American Revolution showed up for their monthly meeting. They took up a long table on the other side of the restaurant, but they weren't being quiet about the topic of their meeting.

Agatha gritted her teeth at the screeching sound of her archenemy's voice. Dot Williams owned the Glamour

Shots and Nail Salon across the street, and she'd decided somewhere along the way to make it her life's mission to get Sheriff Reggie Coil out of office. Since Agatha and Coil were good friends, and she didn't particularly care for people spewing lies and being obnoxious in general, there had been a small confrontation in the salon that had led to a lot of yelling, and the possibility of a middle finger thrown in Dot's direction. Though no one could prove it, and she was sticking by that.

"It's time for a change in this county," Dot said, her voice carrying across the restaurant. "As a longstanding Daughter of the American Revolution, and weekend volunteer down at The Rusty Gun War Heroes and Good Citizen's Memorial Cemetery, we deserve an explanation. This place has gone to hell in a handbasket. Criminals and looting all over the place. And who's fault is it?" She didn't give anyone a chance to answer. "Our very own Sheriff Coil, of course. The most incompetent man I've ever met."

Agatha felt the rage bubbling inside of her. She should've cancelled her breakfast with Heather. Her mood had been volatile. Whether it was hormones or something else, there was something simmering inside of her that she couldn't explain, and it made her all the more angry.

Several of Dot's DAR sisters cheered her on and clapped in agreement.

"Who let that lunatic in here?" Agatha asked, letting her voice carry just like Dot was doing.

Heather laughed, but she shifted in her seat, looking a little nervous.

"Lunatic?" Dot screeched, coming over to stand near their table. The whole restaurant was staring at her now. "Your sheriff is allowing grave robbers to ruin this town's proud historic heritage. Maybe that outlaw gang he associates with don't care about that kind of thing, but we're law abiding citizens here in Rusty Gun, and we expect our elected officials to be the same."

"Are you taking our order?" Heather asked Dot. "I'll take the pancakes. Extra syrup."

Dot scowled at Heather. "Why don't you go find another husband to kill?"

Heather started to come to her feet. "Why don't you kiss my…"

"Heather," Agatha said, putting her hand on her friend's wrist. "She's not worth it. Running her mouth about this election is probably the only attention she's seen in sixty years."

Dot gasped. "I'm only forty-eight. Who do you think you are, Agatha Harley?"

"I know who I am," Agatha said. "And I'm not trying to ruin a good man's reputation just because I'm shacking up with his opponent. Because that's surely the only reason you'd be supporting Oddie McElroy. The man's dumber than a box of hair."

Agatha didn't know what was wrong with her. This wasn't like her at all, but she couldn't seem to stop it now that the ball had started rolling. She didn't even flinch when Dot's hand snapped out and slapped her across the cheek.

"Don't ever touch me again," Agatha hissed. "I will cut you off at the knees."

"Don't you threaten me," Dot said. "I ain't afraid of you. You think no one can touch you because you're some hot shot writer and sleeping with the entire police department? I've got news for you, sister."

The glass of orange juice was in her hand before she realized it, and she tossed it in Dot's face. "Try me, sister."

"That's enough," Sheriff Coil said.

The place fell dead silent, and Coil's gaze zeroed in on Dot and Agatha in the corner.

"Meeting's over, ladies," he said. "I want you out of here. If you can't have a meeting in a public place without causing a disturbance, then you need to have it on private property."

"Well," Dot said, coming up to her full height. "I never…"

"Now would be a good time to keep your mouth shut and do what you're told," Coil said, giving her a hard look. "Or you'll be having DAR meetings from behind bars."

The ladies at the table scrambled to their feet and rushed out the door. Dot looked like she wanted to argue more, but something in Coil's face must've warned her not to try. She straightened her shoulders and marched past him and out the door.

The waitress rushed over with a cloth and cleaned up the orange juice.

"Sorry about that," Agatha told her.

"It's worth the price of the show," the waitress said, grinning. "She's a terrible tipper. I was kind of hoping you'd deck her."

"Maybe next time," Agatha said.

Coil came up to the table and took off his tattered Stetson, hanging it on one of the hooks that were at the top of each booth.

"What in the world was that about?" Coil asked

"Agatha was protecting your honor," Heather said. Then her gaze moved over to Deputy Karl Johnson and warmed. Agatha hadn't even seen Karl come in. "Look at my little brown bear. So handsome."

Karl grinned and took the hand Heather had held out to him, and Agatha rolled her eyes and shared a pained look with Coil.

"Dot said something about a grave robbery over at the cemetery," Agatha said. "And then she said something about you being corrupt and not law-abiding and then she slapped me, so I threw juice in her face. I really wanted to break her face though."

"Well, if she slapped you first then this would've been the time to do it," Coil said.

"I know you're not worried about the politics," Agatha said. "But if historic graves are being desecrated, then Dot's going to be able to get people riled up."

Coil waved a hand in dismissal. "There's a lot of time left before the election. I was on my way to meet Hank here for breakfast when I saw an MMA fight breaking out."

"Hold on a sec," Heather said, raising her index finger. "If y'all are about to talk shop, then I'm out of here. I've had enough of the police for one lifetime."

"What about Karl?" Agatha said, chuckling.

"Oh, he doesn't count," she said. "He's my little brown bear. Besides, when we play cops and robbers, he lets me use the cuffs."

Coil cringed and shot Karl a look, and if it had been possible for Karl to blush, he would've been the color of a tomato.

"You're on duty," Coil said. Karl clearly needed the reminder.

"Come on, sugar buttons," Heather said, scooting out of the seat. "You can walk me to my car."

Coil sighed and rubbed a finger against his temple. "Running a police department is very similar to running a daycare. It's like dealing with children all day long, only the children I'm dealing with carry firearms."

"Which is a comforting tidbit of knowledge," Agatha said.

Her attention was caught by Hank coming through the front door, and she stopped and stared as he made his way across the room. For a big man, he moved like a ghost. Agatha always got a kick out of how people stopped talking and stared at him. There was something about Hank's presence that was intimidating, and most people shied away from him, but she was drawn to him.

"Good morning," Hank said, scooting into the booth next to Agatha. "What'd I miss? I just passed a bunch of women on the street who are mad as hornets. I thought for a second they were going to start a riot."

"Don't discount that option quite yet," Coil said.

"I'm not going to be so nice next time," Agatha said. "I should've decked her." She needed to go home. Her emotions had already been churning, and Dot had just made things worse.

"Come on now, Aggie," Hank teased, "She's done nothing to you but choose another candidate for Reggie's job."

"You can be blasé about it now, but it'll be a different story when your boy here is out of a job come May."

"Thanks for the vote of confidence," Coil said, taking a sip of his piping hot black coffee.

"You know what I mean," Agatha said, waving her hand. "People like Dot Williams and Oddie McElroy don't play fair. It'll be a down and dirty election. Never mind all that. Why don't you tell me what's going down at the graveyard?"

"Looks like we had some vandals who got carried away with two of the gravesites," Coil said. "They dug the coffins up and looted them."

"You still thinking it was high schoolers?" Hank asked.

"Not sure," Coil replied. "It's kind of close to Christmas, so burglaries increase. It's not uncommon for people to look for valuables to steal and pawn, but I don't know if that's what this is."

"Can you see the skeletons?" Agatha asked, fascinated.

"Sure can," Coil said. "You're talking the eighteen sixties, so there's not a whole lot left in there."

Agatha's imagination ran wild with story ideas. "I'd love to see them."

"I'm heading out there after breakfast," Hank said. "You're welcome to come with me as long as…"

"As long as what?" she asked.

"As long as you promise not to punch anyone in the face," he said. "Maybe you've had too much coffee this morning."

"There's no such thing," Agatha said, and took another sip.

Chapter Two

THE RUSTY GUN WAR HEROES AND GOOD CITIZEN'S Memorial Cemetery was located a few miles outside of the city limits, and it had been designated as a national historic site when a grouping of headstones had been discovered by a farmer on his property.

The headstones belonged to five men who'd fought and died at the Alamo. It was tough luck for the farmer to lose his land, but a great opportunity to put Rusty Gun on the map, even if it was the historical map of Texas that almost no one ever read.

Almost a hundred years later, the farmer's land now held hundreds of graves. Agatha loved cemeteries. Each and every headstone told a story.

She fidgeted with the zipper on her windbreaker as Hank parked next to the two patrol cruisers just off the gravel road. She was still in the yoga pants and t-shirt she'd worn to meet Heather for breakfast, but at least the yoga pants were black, and the windbreaker made her look a little less like someone who'd just rolled out of bed and put her hair in a ponytail.

She had a routine in the mornings—wake up, go for a run to help clear the cobwebs, drink coffee in the shower to keep clearing the cobwebs, and then throw on whatever clothes were at the top of the pile and the most comfortable to write in. It's a system that had worked for her for years. But sometimes she had to go out in public.

The five historic graves were in the far southwest corner of the cemetery, and surrounded by a thick copse of pecan trees, which was why it had taken the farmer decades to discover them.

The November air was cool, and there were more cops in the area than she thought were employed.

"I've visited this cemetery twice a month since I moved here," Hank said, "and I never knew this place existed."

Agatha nodded. "I grew up here, and I'd forgotten these graves were here until Coil mentioned them. I think I saw them once when I was a kid, but I didn't have much interest in the significance back then."

Deputies Joe Springer and Jimmie James were standing just on the outside of the barrier they'd created around the gravesites, and she and Hank walked toward them.

"What do you think?" Hank asked them.

James blew out a breath. Despite the cool temperatures, sweat beaded on his upper lip. "It ain't high school kids," he said.

"How you figure?" Hank asked.

Jimmie James was an experienced cop, but he'd bounced around between about as many agencies as he had years under his belt. He found his first troubles with the Houston Police Department, but his natural street instincts made him a valuable pickup for any department that would tolerate him.

"I worked on a burglary task force back in Houston, so I know the tools of the trade. Whoever

LILIANA HART & SCOTT SILVERII

made those markings on the coffin knew what they were doing," James said. "I've seen better, but I've also seen the wreck that high school vandals make. Those scrapings ain't from pranksters. They're from pros."

"Good catch," Hank said."

James nodded, pleased. "I'm off-duty and about to head home, but don't hesitate to call if you need anything." James rambled off and went to let Coil know he was clocking out.

"How about you, Springer?" Hank asked.

Springer was in his mid-twenties, and in looks, he was the exact opposite of James's rugged disposition. Blistering Texas summers took some getting used to, but Hank didn't know how Springer survived them with his soft, pale skin and ginger buzz cut.

"I've been on duty since this morning" Springer said, "but other than the disturbance over at the cafe I haven't heard anything much about this. Didn't figure it was that big of a deal, or everyone would've been talking about it already."

"See anything suspicious on your patrol this morning?" Hank asked. "Maybe a car or a van? A naked guy on horseback?"

Springer wasn't the brightest bulb in the box, and Hank had a feeling his days at the sheriff's office were numbered. Springer looked at him with a perplexed expression, his forehead wrinkling in thought. Hank was surprised smoke wasn't coming out of his ears.

"Oh yeah," Springer said. "I saw a guy on a bike." He grinned, obviously proud of himself.

"A bicycle?" Hank asked.

"No," Springer said. "One like you ride. A Honda."

"It's Harley," Hank said.

"Yes, sir," Springer said, nodding. "I see Ms. Harley right there."

"No, the motorcycle is a Harley Davidson."

"Ha," Springer said. "Just like y'all. Did you ever think about that?"

"No, I never realized," Hank said. "What did the guy on the motorcycle look like?"

"He was ugly."

Hank had never met a cop with as little investigative skills as Springer, and he shook his head.

"You've been a big help, Springer," Hank said and walked away before he strangled the guy. He was grateful Springer was Coil's problem and not his own. Hank would've fired the guy on the spot if he'd been assigned to his task force, but he was no longer in charge. Thank God.

Hank walked beneath the shaded area and ducked under the crime scene tape. Only two of the five graves were disturbed, and the coffins had been well made and of good quality to have lasted so long with little deterioration.

The algae-covered, dark-gray headstones were hard to make out in the shaded grove. He popped out a small flashlight from his pocket and flashed a beam across the hand-engraved stones.

"Figured it out?" Hank asked Agatha.

"I think so," Agatha said, kneeling closer to the open casket on the very end of the row. "Someone dug up these two graves."

Hank snorted out a laugh.

"It doesn't seem like high school kids," she said. "It's not like grave robbing is really on the list of school traditions. Toilet papering and writing on cars in shoe polish, but not desecrating graves."

"See anything else?" he asked.

"Tool scratches on the edges of the casket and beneath

LILIANA HART & SCOTT SILVERII

the lid look like they were made with professional tools, and they were careful not to damage the material. These caskets are a work of art. They would've been very expensive back in that time period."

Hank was impressed. "Did you speak with Deputy James earlier?" he asked.

"No, I saw y'all talking and didn't want to interrupt," she said. "Why?"

"He had the same observations, but he also worked in a specialized burglary task force and knew what to look for. You on the other hand, unless there's a history of being a very sexy cat burglar, are on fire this morning."

"And what does that mean?"

"You start the day with breakfast and a fight, and now you're deciphering clues to a crime scene. On fire."

"It's been a full day," she said, rolling her eyes. "I'll need to go home and take a nap before too much longer."

"What's got you so on edge?" he asked, seeing the flash of anger in her eyes. Something was brewing inside her, and he had no idea what it was.

"People messing with my friends and my town," Agatha snarled. "I'm just sick of it. And I'm not going to sit back and stay silent anymore."

Hank only nodded. He didn't think it was that at all. There was something much deeper bothering Agatha. "You're right about the markings from professional burglary tools. Whoever lifted this lid wanted to make sure there was no damage. But the question is, why be so careful only to leave the lid off and the skeletal remains exposed?"

"Because they weren't trying to conceal the theft," Agatha said. "They got whatever it is they came for."

"I wonder what was in there," Hank said, waving his light around the inside of the first open coffin.

"Whatever it was had to be historic and valuable," Agatha said. "We'll figure it out soon enough."

"I'm sorry, ma'am," a deep voice said behind Agatha. "But neither of you will be figuring anything out about this case. This is now under the jurisdiction of the FBI's historic preservation section's authority. And you need to vacate the premises."

"Excuse me?" Agatha asked, turning around.

Hank winced. Deciding not to sit back and stay silent anymore wasn't the best tactic to take with the FBI.

The agent in question was a modern-day giant. He had to be close to seven feet tall. His skin was black as midnight, and he was dressed in a simple black suit, pressed white shirt and a black tie—standard FBI issue—and he held a leather wallet with a bright gold badge in his hand.

Hank, who stood a solid six feet-two inches had to crane his neck to look up at the official credentials. He'd recognized the man's voice before he'd turned to look at him, and it had been years since he'd seen him.

"Is there a reason you're still standing there?" the agent asked. "What don't you understand? This is a federal historic site, and we are now in charge."

"And how did the FBI happen to hear about two graves being unearthed in the middle of nowhere?" Agatha asked. "Seems a little suspicious to me."

"We received a call from a concerned citizen. The president of the historical society was worried more historic graves would be destroyed before anything was done to stop it."

"Dot," Agatha growled.

"That's her," the agent said. "And apparently she's right to be concerned because you're out here tramping on my crime scene."

"I don't *tramp* anywhere," Agatha said. "I know what I'm doing, and I was invited here by the sheriff. I've probably got more investigative skills in the tip of my finger than an FBI suit that sits at a desk all day."

Hank's eyes just about fell out of his head. Agatha must have lost her mind. If she wasn't careful, they'd all end up in trouble.

"Oh really?" the agent asked. "Why don't you show me your badge, and we'll go from there."

"Show him our badge, Hank," she said, and Hank just closed his eyes and shook his head. Lost her mind. That was the only explanation. But he came up from the crouched position where he'd been watching the show and put himself between Agatha and the agent.

"Hello Sam," Hank said, holding out a hand in greeting.

The man's once granite stone expression lit up with a giant smile as he took the offered hand.

"Hammerin Hank Davidson," he said, pulling Hank into a one-armed hug.

"How ya been?" Hank asked.

"Not too bad," Sam said. "I thought you were retired."

"Wait a second," Agatha said. "You know each other?"

"Aggie, this is Sam Jakes. He and I started out at the Philly PD together," Hank said. "He was smart enough to escape full-time to the FBI. It's been years. And I did retire," he added.

Jakes shoved his credentials back in his pants pocket and reached down to shake her hand. Agatha took it tentatively.

"Man," Jakes said. "It's like you fell off the planet. No one at the bureau has a clue where you went off to. The guys miss you."

"I needed the space," Hank said. "Tell them I miss them too."

"I understand, but the bureau could sure use you. Ain't nobody tracked down killers like Hammerin Hank," Jakes said.

"It turns out I'm still of use around here," Hank said. "Coil appointed me as special investigative detective."

"Not this time, buddy," Jakes said.

"I beg your pardon?" Hank asked, shocked.

"Best thing y'all can do is head home and let me get to work. The FBI doesn't need local help on this."

"Are you serious?" Hank asked, the first hint of anger coming into his voice.

"Dead serious."

Chapter Three

"WHAT THE HECK'S GOING ON?" HANK DEMANDED FROM Coil a little while later.

Agatha paced inside the small office. She thought she'd been angry earlier with Dot, but now she was boiling.

"Y'all need to simmer down," Coil said, and made a time-out sign with his hands.

"Simmer my butt," Agatha shouted. "That's our scene and this is our town. The FBI has no right to sweep in and take over."

"Well," Coil said. "Actually, they do. And they have. There's nothing much we can do about it."

"That witch Dot Williams called them," Agatha said. "That woman is a menace. You should lock her up."

"As soon as she breaks the law, I'm happy to," Coil said.

"Then I'm going over to Glamour Shots to give her a piece of my mind," Agatha said.

"Then I'd have to lock you up," Coil warned.

"Oh really?" she said, tears clouding her eyes. "You're going to arrest me?"

"Agatha," Hank said. "Baby, what's going on? You really need to calm down. This isn't like you at all."

"And what's wrong with the way I am?" she yelled. She couldn't seem to control herself. She was just so…angry. Tears streamed down her face.

"There's nothing wrong with the way you are. But it's not even noon and you've tried to start a fight, tangle with an FBI agent, and now you're daring Coil to throw you in jail."

"At least I'm doing something," she said. "You let Jakes send you off of the scene like a puppy with his tail between his legs."

"Wow," Hank said, brows raising almost to his hairline.

"That's uncalled for," Coil said, trying to restore the peace.

"I think it's time I head home," Hank said, heading for the door. "Call me if you need anything."

Agatha regretted her words, but she had so much anger built up inside she couldn't control what she was saying. She didn't watch him walk out the door.

"That was a low blow," Coil said. "There's nothing that man did to deserve that."

"He should've told that agent where to stick it," she said, and then let out a defeated sigh and dropped into a chair. "It's not fair."

"You talking about the law or your life?" Coil asked.

Agatha just looked at him. The anger had left, and now she felt empty inside.

"I had a visit yesterday from a very nice lady," Coil said. "She works for the office of child welfare."

Big, fat tears dropped onto her lap. She'd bottled up all the feelings that had come after giving up her daughter for adoption. But recently, she'd struggled more with the idea of reconnecting with the daughter she'd never known, especially now that her attacker was dead. She thought it was time to close her life's circle by uniting the pieces that had been shattered by violence.

"I made an inquiry for information a few weeks ago," she confessed. "I wanted to see how the process worked and how to get it started. I didn't realize they'd actually begin the background check."

"Yes," Coil said. "But it'll be your final decision before the woman from child services reaches out to the adoptive parents. This is going to be a tough call, and you'll need the people who love you most to be there for you. Pushing them away right now isn't the best way to move forward."

Agatha wiped the tears from her cheeks. "I know you're right. I'll call him later."

"You should call him now," Coil encouraged. "I know that man, and you cut him deep. His pride is grounded in his work."

She had to get a handle on her emotions. They were both right. This wasn't like her at all.

"Thanks for putting up with me," Agatha said.

"We're friends. It's not about putting up with you. It's about being there to support you and tell you the truths you may not want to hear."

She got up from the chair and gave Coil a quick hug. "I'm going, I'm going," she said.

When she left the sheriff's office, she made sure to put on her sunglasses to cover her red eyes, and then ran across the street to the Taco and Waffle. It was packed.

"There never used to be a line in here," Agatha said, looking toward the front of the line to see how many people were in front of her.

"Come on, people," she snarled. She tucked the loose strands of hair beneath her ball cap.

"Would you like to go before me?" said the cultured,

British voice of the man standing in front of her. "You seem to be in a hurry, and I don't mind. Truly."

Agatha had that deer in the headlights stare as she looked at him. He was her height and wore a tailored, pinstriped suit in dark navy, and she could see her reflection in the shine of his shoes. His hair was curly and dishwater blond, and he wore tortoiseshell glasses. She'd always hated those glasses.

"Agatha?" the man asked. "Agatha Harley? Is that you?"

She hesitated before taking off her sunglasses, but she knew she had to make sure it was him. Maybe she was having an out of body experience. Maybe she was dead, and this was some kind of purgatory.

Her mouth went dry as dust, but she managed to croak out, "Andrew?"

"In the flesh," he said, his smile toothy.

"No," she said, shaking her head. "Nope, nope, nope."

Agatha spun around and bumped into an older couple behind her before rushing back out the door.

Chapter Four

Agatha stood in the hot shower until she was warm and pruney. The bathroom had been remodeled and updated, and it was her sanctuary. She could sit for hours on the bench in the shower and let the hot jets beat against her body. There was no phone, computer, or contact with the outside world. It was her place to think.

She'd come to the conclusion the best course of action was to leave town for a few days. Agent Jakes certainly didn't need her, and Hank…well, Hank was mad at her and had every right to be. He'd ignored her phone calls after she'd left the Taco and Waffle. And then there was the fact that Andrew was in town. That was a whole other problem she didn't want to face. There was nothing in this world that would convince her that her ex-fiancé was in Rusty Gun by chance. Leaving town was the right choice.

"Aggie," Hank yelled, banging on the bathroom door three times before shoving it open.

Agatha let out a screech and slipped off the bench onto the shower floor.

"Are you out of your mind?" she screamed.

"She's in here," Hank yelled into the hallway. "She's code four." Then he turned back to her. "We've been calling and banging on your door for the last hour."

"And?" she asked. "I'm not allowed to be alone in my own house?"

"Coil said you were upset, and then some people at the Taco and Waffle said you'd run out of there like you'd seen a ghost. We were worried."

"So, when I tried to call you earlier and you didn't answer, you're telling me what I should've done was invade your privacy and talk to you whether you wanted to or not."

Hank flushed red.

"Let me tell you something, Hank Davidson. I'm a grown woman. I don't need a babysitter. And until you're looking for something more permanent than what we have, you don't have any rights when it comes to what I do with my time."

His face went stony, and she knew she'd pushed a button. "You already hurt me once today," he said, "but I'm not going to stand around and be kicked like someone's dog."

He slammed the bathroom door and left her alone.

Agatha turned up the sauna and sat back on the marble bench. Tears mixed with the water. She and Hank never fought. Or hardly ever. She needed to apologize, even though he'd been totally out of line storming into her house.

Agatha's hair was still wet when she pulled it all back into a ponytail. She threw on a pair of grey sweatpants and a purple t-shirt that read, "Sorry I'm late, I didn't want to come." She smeared a dab of moisturizer over her forehead and cheeks and headed out the door and hustled over to Hank's house.

She banged on the front door. "Hank, I know you're in there." She used the spare key he'd given her and opened the door.

"Don't shoot," she said. "It's me."

He was sitting in his recliner, staring at the T.V., and doing his best to ignore her.

"I know I hurt you this morning," she said. "I'm sorry."

Silence.

Hank wasn't a man who showed his emotions. He guarded them, and she'd known that long before they'd become a couple. Apologies weren't always enough when male pride was involved.

"I need to tell you why I've been behaving like I have," she said.

"No need," Hank said, coldly. "Coil told me about the visit from the adoption services. You should've come to me. I can see why your emotions are going crazy, but I can't understand why you'd take it out on me."

"Because people lash out at those they're closest to and love the most. It's human nature. And I've told you I'm sorry and meant it. Whether you forgive me or not is up to you."

She turned to leave the house and go back home, but his question stopped her.

"What upset you at the Taco and Waffle? One of the people who saw you leave said there was a man who upset you."

She hesitated, trying to figure out how to explain Andrew to Hank.

"I was upset," she said, nodding. "But I was already upset before I saw him. He was just the straw that broke the camel's back."

"Why?"

"Because we used to be engaged."

"What?" Hank asked, springing out of his chair.

"The key phrase is used to be," Agatha said.

Hank just stared at her. He was doing that a lot. He pivoted sharply on his heel and walked into the kitchen, grabbing an Ensure from the fridge and a banana from the bowl, and he went out to the back porch.

She almost let him go. He had every right to be mad, and maybe he just needed space. But there was give and take, and she was hurting too. Two wrongs didn't make a right, and she could've used a little compassion from Hank.

Agatha marched through the kitchen and out onto the patio.

"We've both been hurt today," she said, "but I'm not leaving until we are back on solid ground."

He just bit into the banana and chewed fiercely.

"I care about you, and although we don't talk much about it, I love you and need you to be here for me right now."

"If you really needed me you would've told me about the adoption agency sooner," he said.

"I've spent almost my entire life alone," she said. "I'm used to relying on myself, and only myself. We've been serious almost a year. Trusting someone else and relying on someone else isn't second nature. Just like it's not second nature for you. But you giving me the cold shoulder instead of trying to hear things from my point of view isn't going to make things better. I was already upset about whether or not to push forward in finding my daughter and reconnecting. Then there was Dot, the fight with Agent Jakes, and then you…then Bacon waltzes into town, and he's the last person I wanted to see. I'd talked myself into leaving town for a few days when you barged into my bathroom."

"Who is Bacon?" he asked, still not making eye contact.

"Andrew," she said between clenched teeth. "My ex-fiancé. People call him Bacon."

"And what is he doing in Rusty Gun?"

"I have no idea," she said. "The last I'd heard he'd taken a research position at Scotland Yard. I haven't seen or heard from him in years."

"Scotland Yard?" Hank asked.

"Yep," she said. "He's the world's most renowned forensic anthropologist, and the only reason I could think for him to be here is if he's been called in for a special assignment."

"Andrew?" Hank asked again, his expression quizzical. He finally looked at her. "Are you talking about Dr. Andrew Lawrence? *The* Dr. Lawrence."

"Yes," she said.

"Aggie, I didn't just fall fresh off the turnip truck. The FBI is not going to call in someone like Dr. Lawrence because a grave was opened and a few trinkets were stolen. And another question, if he is here because of the grave robberies, we only found out about it this morning. He didn't just take a time machine from London and get here in time for the investigation. He's been in the area."

"Maybe it's an ongoing case?" she suggested. "Does it matter? We're off the case anyway, so it's not our problem. And even if we were on the case, I could just pass on it."

"Why? Can't trust yourself around him?" he asked.

"Really?" she asked. "That's the direction you're going to take this?"

"Why not?" he said. "We've known each other for two years, and never once, not once have you ever mentioned that you'd been engaged. And now he just shows up out of the blue, and I'm supposed to be okay with it?"

"Maybe I didn't mention it because it was literally that unimportant to me," she said, her voice rising. "I seem to recall it was more than a *year* before you bothered to tell me you'd been married before, so how about you not throw stones at glass houses. Or maybe you're fine with me confiding in you about every aspect of my life, like you were just complaining about with the adoption agency, but you don't feel the rules should reciprocate?

"But, hey," she said, "If you're ready to start telling me about your past and your old cases, and all of the other stuff I know you keep hidden inside like some kind of badge of honor, I'm all ears."

Hank remained stone-faced and silent.

"Yeah, that's what I thought," she said, and turned on her heel and escaped through the back gate.

Chapter Five

THE BELL COUNTY SHERIFF'S OFFICE WASN'T BIG ENOUGH to hold Agent Jakes's body or Dr. Lawrence's enormous ego. He wasn't sure why Coil had called him into the office, but the meeting was keeping him from thinking about Agatha.

Hank scanned Coil's office and took in the presence of Jakes and Lawrence, but he didn't acknowledge them. He shook Coil's hand and said, "What's going on?"

Hank and Jakes might have gone back a way, but the way he'd been dismissed from the crime scene was a complete disregard for professional courtesy.

"Thanks for coming, Hank," Coil said. From what I understand, you already know Special Agent Sam Jakes?"

"I do," Hank said.

"And this is Dr. Andrew Lawrence," Coil went on.

Hank tamped down the urge to strangle the man and extended his hand instead. "Nice to meet you."

"So, you're the famous Hammerin Hank," Lawrence said, awe lacing his proper British voice. "I've read so many of your briefs that I feel I already know you. You were quite an asset to the FBI."

"Thank you." Hank said. He could see the amusement on Coil's face, and he was glad at least one of them was getting a kick out of this encounter. And if he had to guess, Coil probably knew exactly who this Lawrence guy was to Agatha. Coil and Agatha had grown up in the same town. They had memories that Hank would never be a part of.

Lawrence was a slender man, and several inches shorter than Hank. He was well dressed in a suit more expensive than Hank would've ever considered wasting his money on, and his shoes were shined so they looked like mirrors.

Coil cleared his throat and looked at Hank. If Hank wasn't mistaken, it was embarrassment on Coil's face. "Is your fiancé going to join us?" Coil asked.

Hank kept his face passive and didn't let his surprise show. "I'm not sure. Agatha said her plate was pretty full today."

"Agatha?" Lawrence asked, jumping on the name.

Hank and Coil exchanged glances.

"Yes," Hank said. "Agatha Harley."

"The author?"

"Yes, you've heard of her?"

Lawrence's already sallow complexion paled even more.

"And she's your fiancé?" he asked.

"Last time I checked," Hank said, finding a smile for the first time. The smile must not have been very reassuring because Lawrence took a step back. "You know her?"

"Hmm," Lawrence said, and then dropped his gaze.

Hank looked back at Coil. In all honesty, he just wanted to go back home. He didn't care about the graves, the FBI, or the fact that he was only in the office because someone probably wanted something from him.

"So, what's going on since I was dismissed from the crime scene?" Hank asked. "I assume that's why I'm here?"

"It seems like the FBI would appreciate your assistance," Coil said.

"I'm not sure that's an option, Sheriff," Hank said. "You see, Mr. Jakes over there made no bones about it. I was not to set foot on his crime scene."

Jakes looked away, but in the tiny office, there wasn't much space for even wandering glares.

"Well, it seems that the FBI has changed its position on getting local assistance," Coil said. "And, as a duly commissioned representative of my office, I am requesting your assistance in granting them the local guidance they so desperately need."

"In other words, they can't find their butts with both hands because no one will give them the time of day except for Dot Williams. Am I right?"

"That pretty much sums it up." Coil's smile was sharp.

"Can I get back to you on that request?" Hank said. "I left Agatha in a hurry. She was upset about a run-in she had over at the Taco and Waffle."

"Oh, that would be me," Lawrence said, much too cheerfully for Hank's taste.

"Yeah, I had a feeling," Hank said with a snarl. "Catch you later."

"Wait a second, Hank," Jakes called out. "Where are you going?"

"Home."

"Can I talk to you?" Jakes asked, unfolding long legs and coming to a standing position. "Outside?"

"Sure," Hank said. "I'm heading that direction anyway."

Hank stepped out of the sheriff's office and breathed in the fresh air, and then turned so his back was to the sun. Jakes followed him through the door and they squared off, but Jakes took the full brunt of the bright sun to his face. He shielded his eyes with his hand, but Hank didn't move.

"Look," Jakes said. "We go way back. I shouldn't have said what I said. I was a little surprised to see you out there. I guess when it came down to it, my concern was that I'd have to compete with you for authority."

"I like you, Sam," Hank said. "And we do go back a long way. I've never blamed you for Tammy's death, but you weren't there when the team needed you the most. Even after all this time, knowing the kind of cop I am, worrying about who's in charge is your top priority? And now you need me because the people in this town won't talk to an outsider, even if you do have a fancy badge."

"I didn't say I was right," Jakes said. "And I've apologized a thousand times for the night Tammy died. I accepted my transfer out of violent crimes and into the boring world of white-collar crime. But I can't keep beating myself up over what happened to your wife. We've both got to move forward at some point."

Hank's heart remained heavy. The reality that Hank wasn't the only person who still carried pain over the loss of his wife made the burden seem not so unbearable. Maybe that was what was on his mind when he'd argued with Agatha. Seeing Jakes and then being dismissed like a child hurt more personally than it did professionally. But in the end, Hank was a cop's cop, and there was a crime to solve.

"You're right, Sam," Hank said. "But it's still no reason for the way you treated me this morning. I'll help because

Sheriff Coil asked me to, and because this is my hometown. It has zero to do with you, the Bureau, or that snob you brought along."

Jakes held up his hands. "Fair enough. And for the record, I didn't bring the snob. He was already in the Dallas Field Office when the call came in. One of the group supervisors wanted to get rid of him, so they shoved him off on me. He doesn't belong to the FBI, but he's in very good with the Deputy Director and several other key players."

"And he's the best," Hank said.

Jakes sighed. "And that too. Apparently, he's taking a sabbatical for several weeks and decided to grace us with his presence while he does research."

"Convenient," Hank said.

Jakes held out his hand to Hank. "Are we good?" he asked.

Hank waited a beat before he accepted the offered hand. "Yeah, we're good."

Chapter Six

AGATHA STARED OUT THE SIDE WINDOW OF HANK'S BMW. He'd stopped by the house and explained that Jakes had asked them to come back on in a consultant capacity, and he'd also told her that Lawrence had chosen the area to take his sabbatical. Between that and the fact that Hank was acting like their argument had never happened, she was reluctant to go back to the cemetery with him. She also wasn't too keen on facing Jakes again either after their earlier interaction, but she was willing to put it behind her for the sake of solving a good mystery.

It was mid-afternoon, but Coil had ordered bright mobile light stands on scene for when dusk began to fall. The place had been guarded like King Tut's tomb all day long, and there was a definite hostility in the air between the local cops and the Feds.

"Are you sure it's okay to be here, or will you throw us out again?" Agatha asked Jakes good-naturedly.

Jakes grinned and held out his hand to shake hers. "I do apologize, ma'am," Jakes said. "I promise to be on my best behavior."

She saw Lawrence come up behind Jakes, and she felt her smile go stiff. Lord, she had no idea why she'd ever been engaged to the man, much less why she even dated him. She'd been lonely was her best guess, and she'd been getting to that age where she'd been thinking of marriage and children. And he was brilliant in his field. But he'd bored her to death. He'd also annoyed her endlessly. Needless to say, their engagement had been very short."

"Hello, Agatha," Lawrence said. "It's lovely to see you again. You can imagine how surprised I was to see you in the restaurant today."

"Yes," she said, narrowing her eyes. "Very surprising."

"I apologize if I alarmed you."

"You didn't," she said. "What are you doing here?"

"Special Agent Jakes requested my assistance on this investigation," he said, shrugging. So here I am. I assure you; it was completely coincidental."

"Hmm," she said, but she felt herself relax some. It was a specialized field, and these skeletal remains were definitely unusual. It would make sense they'd want someone with his skill."

Lawrence looked at her slyly—a completely British look that only someone with his level of snobbery could pull off. "Oh, by the by," he said. "Congratulations are in order for your engagement. I had the chance to meet your Mr. Davidson. Of course, I've spent years reading his case files. He's quite brilliant."

"Yes, he is," she said, and left it at that.

"Okay, team," Coil said, calling everyone together. "We're going to be cooperating with the FBI and the state's historic preservation society to make sure that we not only solve this crime, but that we protect our great history and heroes."

Agatha barely kept from rolling her eyes. Coil was

laying it on thick for the outsiders and the media. It was all part of the political game. Fortunately, it was Coil up there and not her. Diplomacy wasn't a virtue she possessed.

She moved closer to Hank and spoke in a low voice so only he could hear. "What's your take on this?"

"Too soon to tell," he said. "But I'm very interested in the biker Deputy Springer saw in the area."

"You think the Rattlers are still looking to get back at you?" she asked.

"Sure, but I don't think it's connected to this. It's just something to tuck away for later."

"I'm going to hand this over to Agent Jakes," Coil said.

"Thank you, Sheriff," Jakes said. "We're all here to do the job. The most important thing is that we find who did this and recover what was taken from these historic graves. So put your egos behind you and get the job done. The CSI team has finished processing the immediate area around the graves for footprints or other evidence, so you're clear to move within the perimeter. Sheriff Coil and I are both here for questions if you have any."

"That's our cue," Hank said.

"For what?" Agatha asked.

"To get answers to a few questions that have been rattling in my brain since this morning."

"You too?" she asked.

"Yes," Hank said, looking at her oddly. "But I'm interested to hear what's been on yours."

Agatha took a deep breath and put her hands on her hips. "I always thought these gravesites were memorials to the heroes who fought and died at the Alamo," Agatha said. "It's not until today that I realized they're actual graves with the real soldiers buried in them."

"Why's that a problem?" Hank asked, staring at the remains in one of the caskets.

33

"Because it says on the headstones that these men fought and died at the Alamo."

"I'm still not seeing why this is a problem," Hank said.

"Because it's well documented in history that General Santa Anna's army of four thousand slaughtered the one hundred and eighty rebels fighting for Texan independence. And after the dust settled, Santa Anna's men piled all of the bodies up and burned them in three funeral pyres. It burned for days, and there are no records of any bodies being returned to their families, much less five of them," she said, pointing to the line of graves.

"Yeah, that's definitely a red flag," Hank said. "There's something else suspicious. Have you noticed?"

"You're quite right, Detective Davidson," Lawrence said, coming up behind them.

Agatha gasped in surprise, but Hank just gave Lawrence a look to let him know he was definitely intruding.

"I'm sure you've both noticed by now that the skeletal remains in both coffins are female."

Lawrence's voice hadn't been soft when he made the announcement, and a group gathered around to hear what he had to say.

"Yes," Agatha said, annoyed on Hank's behalf. "Hank was just explaining that to me when you walked up, Bacon."

"Who's Bacon?" Coil asked.

"Oh," Agatha said. "I meant Dr. Lawrence."

Andrew turned pink and cleared his throat. "Just a silly nickname," he said.

"How'd you know it was female?" Coil asked Hank.

"It's hard to tell actually," Hank said, "But males are generally larger, and their bones are thicker with sharp corners. That in itself doesn't exclude females, but what really sets them apart…"

"Is the pelvis," Lawrence interrupted, putting his hands at his hips and rotating his pelvis.

"Good grief," Agatha said.

"Nice form, Doc," Coil said. "I bet you do a real good Macarena."

"Beg pardon?" Lawrence asked.

"Never mind," Coil said. "Sorry to interrupt, Hank. Keep going."

"The female's body is built for childbirth. Her pelvic bones are shorter and more rounded, and the tailbone is more flexible to accommodate gestation and child delivery."

"Are you saying my hips are wide?" Agatha asked, raising a brow.

"Your hips are perfect," Hank said.

"I was just thinking that myself," Lawrence said. "You've quite lovely hips. They have an excellent rhythm."

"Shut up, Lawrence," Coil said. "You're standing in front of an open grave. It'd be really easy for Hank to shove you in one."

"Oh, well," Lawrence said, pursing his lips.

"Rally up everyone," Jakes called out. He jumped up on the hood of a cruiser so he could get everyone's attention. "It looks like this has taken an unexpected twist. I've just been informed that Dr. Lawrence will escort both skeletal remains to Austin where he'll be able to examine them in a lab. Preliminarily though, it looks like both remains are female, and are not, in fact the bodies of Major Nathan Hills or Lieutenant Wayne Brush. Because of this fact, this is no longer being treated as an historical preservation site."

"Austin, sir?" Lawrence asked. "Why do I need to go to

Austin? Isn't there somewhere suitable I can work in the area? I'd like to stay close to the scene…" He snuck a look at Agatha that Hank didn't miss. "Just in case."

"Get to work Lawrence," Jakes said. "I want to know who these women are, and if they were put there in place of remains that were stolen. And I wanted answers yesterday."

Chapter Seven

They'd worked past midnight before breaking, and they were all back at it the following morning, only this time they were briefing in the sheriff's office before heading out to the site. Jakes had ditched the suit and tie for tan BDUs and a navy polo emblazoned with FBI over the breast pocket.

"Good morning you two," Coil said to Hank and Agatha. "Better stock up on coffee if you got as much sleep as I did last night."

Agatha had slept like a baby knowing Lawrence was in Austin and would be out of their hair at least for the next little while. And she helped herself to the assortment of pastries that had been donated by the Kettle Café, choosing a berry-filled kolache to start. She could tell Hank also seemed more at ease now that Andrew was out of the picture.

"Morning Sam," Hank said as Jakes walked in. "Anything new since last night?"

"Not that I've heard," he said. "I'm guessing it's going

37

to take the good doctor at least a couple of days to get me some information. I certainly don't expect an I.D."

"The longer he stays gone, the better," Hank said.

Jakes smiled and grabbed a donut from the tray. Agatha should've known he'd go for a plain glazed donut. He didn't seem like the adventurous type.

"The doc has eyes for your lady," Jakes said.

"I noticed," Hank said. "If he comes back too soon you might have a missing person on your hands. He's not being very subtle about it, but I can guarantee he'll be the first to go."

"Understood," Jakes said, biting into his donut. "There shouldn't be any need for him to spend much more time here with us. He's better served in a lab and he knows it."

Agatha should've known it was too good to be true.

"Top of the morning, everyone," Lawrence said cheerfully, bursting through the door with enough enthusiasm that all the armed men in the room had their hand on their weapons. He was wearing the same clothes as the night before, but his tie was missing and his suit jacket was rumpled. His hair was mussed, and there was a strawberry blonde stubble that was barely visible on his cheeks. His eyes were bloodshot, and they had a half-crazed look in them.

"What are you doing here, Lawrence?" Jakes asked. "Unless you have an identity for me of those two remains then you'd best turn around and head straight back to the lab."

Lawrence headed straight for the pastry tray, selected one and put it daintily on a napkin, and then poured himself a cup of coffee. "Quite right, quite right," Lawrence said. "Both remains are, in fact, female, and I can assure you that the remains do not date back to 1836."

"Fantastic," Jakes said. "But that doesn't help us out any here."

"I can also tell you," Lawrence said, steamrolling right through Jakes' comment, "That they are the original inhabitants of those coffins. No bodies were switched at any time, and those particular remains date between ninety and a hundred and ten years old. That also coincides with the brand marking I found on the coffin. Both victims would've been in their early twenties, and neither had given birth."

"Okay," Coil said. "That's a little more helpful."

"So, who are they?" Jakes asked.

"Good question," Lawrence said. "It turns out I only had to move the remains from the coffin to find out." He pulled out an evidence bag, and inside was an ornate locket in silver. "This was found tangled in the hair of the first set of remains. It's got a maker's mark stamped on the back and a photograph of a man and woman together. And an inscription—*To Margaret, with Love.*"

"You were able to find an identity of the victim based on a first name?" Jakes asked.

"Normally, it would be quite difficult," he agreed. "But it seems our Margaret was quite famous. When I typed in the dates of the coffin, the locket, and her name, and then ran the photo through a facial recognition program, I was able to come up with Margaret Scott in no time at all.

"She was quite well-known as a bootlegger, and she went missing when she was twenty-one years old. A body was never found, and she was never heard from again." Lawrence pulled a grainy photograph from his bag and set it on the table, and then carefully opened the locket so they could see the picture inside. It was definitely a match.

"That's good work," Hank said, grudgingly.

"Yes," Lawrence said, agreeing.

"What about her friend?" Jakes asked.

"Well, she was a bit more challenging," Lawrence said, pulling at his ear. "But that's where science was able to lend a helping hand. Our second set of remains was what's commonly known as a hexadactyly."

"And what's that?" Jakes asked.

"It means she had six fingers," Agatha said, jumping in on Lawrence's thunder.

"Quite right," Lawrence said. "And as I kept digging, I found information of a close friendship between Margaret Scott and a Penelope Pennywell. Penelope had quite a reputation in her own right. She was a madam, renowned for her six fingers."

"That is fascinating," Agatha said, already trying to figure out how she could use that in a book.

"The good thing about Mistress Pennywell is that she has descendants in the area still to this day."

"How in the world would you know that?" Coil asked.

"The ancestry sites," Lawrence said. "People are freely giving their DNA for the government to use how they please, and they don't even know they're doing it. It's quite ingenious. And helpful. How do you think we caught the Golden State Killer?"

"Okay, so what about this woman's relatives?" Agatha asked.

"She doesn't have direct descendants," Lawrence said, "but I was able to track down a distant cousin, and I contacted her this morning. She said Aunt Penny was a legend, and they've passed down the stories for generations."

"What happened to her?" Coil asked.

"The family story is that she fell in love with one of her customers, and they ran off together to start a new life. But clearly, Aunt Penny's story ended differently."

Jakes sighed and shook his head, and it was obvious he didn't want to be impressed by Lawrence. "Hank's right. That's good work."

Lawrence practically preened under all the praise.

"So, the question is," Coil said, "Why are these two friends buried next to each other a hundred miles from where they lived? And who's buried in the other three graves?"

"Jolly good questions," Lawrence said.

His chest had puffed out, and he was clearly under the delusion he was in charge at this point. Agatha just shook her head. His ego was only one of the reasons he was best served in small doses.

"I took the liberty of contacting Agent Jakes' field office supervisor, and we should have the exhumation orders for the other graves within the hour."

You could have heard a pin drop in the office, and the tension skyrocketed, but Lawrence was clueless as usual. Hank whistled silently between his teeth.

"Let's take a walk, Lawrence," Jakes said, grabbing the man by the shoulder and pushing him out the door.

"I'm quite tired," Lawrence said. "Maybe we could talk after I've had a bit of shut eye."

Jakes squeezed harder and Lawrence's knees buckled.

"Or now is good."

Chapter Eight

ALL IN ALL, IT WAS GOOD WEATHER FOR GRAVE DIGGING.
Agatha sat on a blanket next to Hank and enjoyed a second
sandwich. The Taco and Waffle had made up a batch of
chicken salad, and they'd treated everyone working the scene.

"What's on your mind," she asked Hank.

"Just wondering how Andrew is sitting," Hank said.
"You got to imagine his behind is on fire after that lashing
Jakes gave him."

"I doubt Bacon even noticed he was getting a lashing.
He tends to live in his own world, and other people's
feelings aren't even a blip on his radar."

"Why do you call him Bacon?" Hank asked.

"His family has called him that since he was a kid
because he's always been somewhat of a nerd. After Sir
Francis Bacon."

"Who?"

"The scientist who developed the scientific method."

"His family must've been a barrel of monkeys. You
spend much time with them?"

"No, but to be fair, I didn't spend much time with him either. Our work was more important than each other, and honestly, I knew I made a mistake from the moment I agreed to marry him. He drove me crazy. He's socially awkward, and he's self-absorbed and selfish. But he's brilliant."

"I guess that's good enough for me," Hank said, finishing his sandwich and wiping his hands on a napkin. "I got a message from Deputy James that he's investigating a burglary that has tool marks similar to what we found on the coffin. It might be worth sneaking out of here and checking it out."

"What about the biker?" Agatha asked.

He sighed. "I don't know. Maybe I'm just projecting, but I've got a feeling in my gut it's not something to overlook. Deputy Springer is as useful as a cop as Lawrence would be in a Judo match. So, it depends on whether the biker was a kid on a Moped or one of the Rattlers on a HOG."

"What would the connection be between these women and the Rattlers?" Agatha asked.

"Money is always a motivator, even back then. And there's a lot of Confederate gold that was never found."

"Huh," Agatha said. "What if those graves are part of a treasure map, and now someone is digging them up so they can hunt for the booty."

"Are we talking about Agatha's hips again?" Lawrence said, taking a seat next to them on the blanket.

"I will stab you with this plastic fork," Agatha said, holding it up so he could see it.

"You've become quite violent," he said, frowning with disapproval. "I don't think I like that. I remember you were always shooting those horrendous guns."

"Yes, and if you mention my hips again, I'll use you as target practice," she said.

"Fine, fine," he said, raising his hands. "I just came to tell you that I've narrowed down the possibilities of the women who might be in the other graves."

"Assuming they're women," Hank retorted.

"Fair enough, old boy. But you've worked enough cases to know that multiple crimes are based on impulse or patterns. It's obvious to see that these five graves were not dug on impulse. It's also a statistically significant probability that the other remains are women."

"Okay," Hank agreed. "So, who are they?"

"I've had my team running multivariate regression models to factor in the same era that these ladies disappeared, other women in the same age grouping, reports of missing, dead, or arrested women in the region, and information from the Social Security Administration's database of the deceased."

"And?" Hank asked.

"I believe I've narrowed it down quite handily. One of the women owned a speakeasy and made sure her customers got all the drinks they wanted. Another was an exotic dancer. She was apparently quite skilled. And the last…" Lawrence smiled slyly. "The last was a nun from the Franciscan community of Poor Clare Nuns of Perpetual Adoration in San Antonio."

"A nun?" Agatha asked. "Why in the world would you narrow it down to a nun? The bootlegger, the madam, the speakeasy owner, and the exotic dancer, I get. But a nun?"

"She's the outlier," Lawrence said.

"Explain in English," Agatha said.

"In quantitative statistics," he said in his best lecture voice, "there are often outliers in the data that can skew the outcome or analysis. There are regiments to account for those factors that sit at the far ends from the average's middle."

"I'm about to fall asleep," Hank said.

Lawrence sunk his teeth into his second chicken salad sandwich. Of course, a dollop of dressing plopped on the crotch of his navy trousers. He looked up with a boyish smirk.

"If five women of questionable character go missing within the same time period, a red flag should go up somewhere. But if you throw in a nun, it evens out the hysteria of a pattern of bad girls gone missing."

"I don't know," Hank said. "It's a stretch considering law enforcement back then in no way had the sophistication to correlate crimes across town much less across the state."

"I totally get it," Agatha murmured. "But there's also a purpose for who they chose. Maybe not by who they were, but what they did. Think about it," she said. "Why would there be a false cemetery hidden for who knows how long out in the middle of nowhere? War heroes that aren't heroes at all. There are dates, names, and unusual etchings on each of the gravestones. They have to mean something. I think they're a map of some sort."

"Oh," Lawrence said, excitement in his voice. "Like a treasure hunt?"

"Treasure?" Jakes asked, stepping up behind them.

"Don't mind her," Hank said. "Her writer's imagination is running wild."

"Oh, yes," Lawrence said. "I remember that imagination well."

"Remember what I said I'd do to you with this fork," Agatha said.

"Goodness gracious," he said, getting to his feet and

then he muttered something about Americans as he wandered off.

Jakes sighed and ran a hand through his head. "He's a pain, but you can't fault his skill."

"No kidding," Hank agreed. "And I've hardly wanted to punch him."

Jakes laughed and then said, "We're going to give everyone a break until the backhoe and truck with the crane arrives from Austin. I can't wait to see what else is in those coffins."

Chapter Nine

AGATHA AND HANK DECIDED TO WAIT AT AGATHA'S HOUSE until the equipment showed up. Mostly, Agatha wanted to do her own research on the names Lawrence had dug up. Margaret Scott and Penelope Pennywise sounded like two fascinating, liberated women from the Roaring Twenties. No way could they have ended up in caskets next to each other in death without running through adventures together in life.

Agatha had been pouring over information on her computer in the war room, and Hank had wandered off into the kitchen.

"Hey, Hank?" she called out.

"What's up?"

"Did the mob monopolize everything during prohibition?" she asked.

Hank didn't answer for several seconds, but she could hear him rattling around in the kitchen. "They did in the big cities, but I'm sure with all of the moonshiners out in the sticks, there were probably a lot of independent operators, especially in the south. Why?"

"It makes sense for a bootlegger, a madam, and the owner of the speakeasy to be in business with each other. But do you think they'd be associated with the mob?"

"Not necessarily," Hank said.

Agatha narrowed her eyes. "What's up with all the short answers? Are you eating the ice cream?"

She peeked around the corner of the kitchen and caught him red-handed. Hank stood over the sink with a pint of Blue Bell chocolate chip cookie dough and a spoon. He just grinned at her unrepentantly.

"I thought you were on a diet?"

"I am," he said. "But when you buy stuff like this, I feel obligated to eat it."

"Does that mean if you have to suffer then I do too?" she asked.

"Pretty much."

"When you're done, maybe you could come help me. I don't think the Lone Star Rattlers are involved in this at all. I think it's mob related."

"Well, that's interesting, except I don't think this area had a big mafia influence in the day," Hank said.

"I just think there's more to it than dead girls and buried treasure."

"Well, if the Rattlers are out of the picture, then I doubt the prize was treasure. Money, war bonds, or monetary instruments would've been the take," Hank said.

"How do you feel about your mystery biker?" she quizzed him.

"Aggie, I've learned that you never discard any ideas, suspicions, or leads. The Rattlers have been around since Texas was its own republic, so don't discount the reality that if there's even as much as a dime to be made off of anything, they'll have their hands in it."

"You're still worried about the bounty they have out on you?" she asked.

"Nah, it's part of the job," Hank said.

"But you're not on the job anymore, Hank. You're retired. I know it bothers you."

"Maybe just a little," he confessed. "But I'm not backing away from them. I live ready," he said, patting his pistol. "Tell me about Margaret and Penelope."

"I'll pull up what I've got," she said, tapping a few keys on the computer so images appeared on the wall screen. Hank took a seat on the chaise. "I found some microfiche and old newspaper clippings."

"Margaret Scott came from a prominent, very religious family. They got their money from oil and had a lot of power in San Antonio. But Margaret was disowned after she started bootlegging. She'd actually been accepted to nursing school and was getting ready to start her first term when she decided there were more lucrative ways to make a living."

"She might have been trying to escape from an overly strict family life. Times were different then. Women didn't have a lot of options."

"I think someone gave her some options and she jumped at the chance to escape. To become her own person and be independent. She was very young."

"What about Penelope Pennywell?"

"I'm just starting on her," Agatha said. "But I think a visit with her family might pay off big time. They live about an hour away from here, and from what I can tell, money has been in the family a long time."

"Oil?" Hank asked.

"Cattle for the most part, but I'm thinking there's oil in there too."

"Why would you think so?" Hank asked.

LILIANA HART & SCOTT SILVERII

An image popped up on the screen. It was from a social media account linked to Penelope's great-grand niece. It was a woman posing with what looked like her kids and grandkids. The family was gathered in an open field, and in the background was an army of land-based oil derrick pumps lined up like rusty grasshoppers.

Agatha flashed her red laser pointer at the oil producers and waggled it for Hank's attention.

"How about that, big boy?" she exaggerated her accent. "There's oil in them there hills."

"You think oil is how the two families knew each other?"

"It's as good of a theory as any," she said. "I've got the names of the other three women. Maybe we can find a connection between all their families."

"We'll have to do it later," Hank said, checking his phone. "Time to get back to the cemetery."

Chapter Ten

A CROWD HAD GATHERED OUTSIDE THE CEMETERY—LOCALS trying to get bits of information about the heroes they thought were buried there. People were going to be fit to be tied once they found out the truth. Rusty Gun didn't have much going for it. The Alamo heroes and the John Wayne statue in the middle of town were pretty much the only tourist attractions for miles.

The line of traffic to get into the cemetery was ridiculous, so he parked the car on the side of the road, and they walked the rest of the way. Hank made sure his badge was visible on his belt, and he waved to Deputy Springer as they crossed the crime scene tape.

"Anything more on that biker you saw earlier?" Hank asked.

"What biker?" Springer said, slapping at a bug on his neck.

Hank blew out a slow breath and tried again. "The guy on the motorcycle you told me about earlier."

"Oh, yeah," he said, grinning. "Haven't given it much thought. We've been pretty busy here."

"Yeah, I can see that," Hank said, smiling tightly.

Agatha waited until they'd walked away before she asked. "Still stuck on the Rattlers?"

"Not really. I was just curious about how serious that kid was about his job," Hank said. "I know the cop out of Dallas that helped us with Buck Hazard's case recently applied for a job. I think she'd make a great addition."

"So, you're making room for her? I thought the sheriff's office couldn't afford to bring on any more deputies."

"They can't, but Deputy Springer is digging his own hole."

The backhoe and crane were already at work on the graves, and Agatha went over to watch the process close up.

"Hey, Jakes," Hank said, coming to stand beside him. "Anything new?"

"Not on my end," he said, keeping his stare straight ahead. "But I hear Agatha has a solid theory about our first two bodies?"

Surprise widened Hank's eyes. He knew darned good and well Agatha hadn't contacted Jakes about any leads. Which meant he was fishing.

"Hey, buddy," Coil said, coming up next to him. "You showed up just in time for the show. What have y'all been doing?"

"What Agatha does best," Hank said. "Research."

The smell of earth was strong as they brought the third coffin up from the ground. The coffin was the same ornate kind as the others with the same seller's mark. A couple of Jakes's men undid the chains around the coffin, and they waited for permission before they attempted to open it.

"Go ahead," Jakes said.

Hank winced as they took a crowbar to the coffin and

lifted the lid. And then he heard Agatha and Lawrence gasp.

"What is it?" Jakes asked.

"Another body," Lawrence said. "Female."

"And a whole heck of a lot of gold and jewels," Agatha said. "Holy smokes, if the first two coffins had this kind of loot, the thieves got off with a fortune."

"If it's real," Jakes said.

"We'll find out soon enough," Lawrence said, clapping his hands together. "Let's get them back to my lab. I can't wait to dig in."

"How about a little respect," Coil said. "There's still a body in there."

"Right-o," he said, but didn't look contrite at all. He looked like a kid on Christmas morning.

"This really complicates matters," Jakes said.

"How so?" Agatha asked.

"Well, if the other two had the same contents, then we're dealing with a lot more than simple grave desecrations. I had already assumed we were dealing with murder, but this amount of money implies robbery and fraud at the least, with the possibility of a much bigger mess."

"I sure am glad the FBI is here to clean up the mess," Coil said.

There was no humor in Jakes's laugh. "Thanks, Coil. I'm going to be stuck on this thing through the holidays. I should've told that Dot Williams to blow it out her tail pipe and contact her local law enforcement."

"That's the breaks, buddy," Coil said, slapping Jakes on the arm good-naturedly. "Need extra manpower bringing these in?" Coil asked.

"Why? Don't think the FBI can handle it?"

Coil adjusted his Stetson cowboy hat on his head. It

had seen better days, but no matter how tattered, it was always ready for duty. Just like Coil.

"Honestly," Coil said. "No. You've got two juniors that look like they've never been out of the office and this guy," he said, jerking a thumb at Lawrence.

"Is that an insult?" Lawrence said. "I'll have you know I'm quite proficient in fencing."

Jakes just closed his eyes and shook his head.

"We know it wasn't amateurs who carted off the first haul." Coil said. "Wouldn't you think whoever cleaned them out is waiting for the opportunity to get the rest?"

"You think there's an active threat in the area?" Jakes asked.

"Don't you?"

"I do," Jakes agreed. "That's why I've got a SWAT team down the road waiting for my signal."

Chapter Eleven

AGATHA HAD ENJOYED WATCHING THE FBI'S SPECIAL operations SWAT unit arrive and take possession of casket number three. She paid particular attention to the way they conducted themselves around reporters, other cops, and the public. They were swift, silent, and as she assumed, deadly.

"You think they'll have time to get the other two up before it gets dark?" Agatha asked.

"Yes, they'll have to," Hank said. "We're in too deep. We've got the lights that Coil brought over yesterday, and I don't think it's wise or safe to abandon the site until everything is done."

"Yeah," Agatha said. "I figured you'd say that."

"Hey, at least Lawrence is out of your hair," Hank said, hugging her around the waist.

"Maybe so, but I'm still cold. I already miss summer."

"Bite your tongue, woman," Hank said. "I'm still not used to that heat. But I can keep you warm if you're cold." He pulled her in tighter.

"I bet Dot would love to watch that," Agatha said,

nodding her head toward the barricade. "Doesn't that haggard woman have a life?"

They were loading the next coffin onto the back of a flatbed truck, and she and Hank moved in that direction.

Agatha heard the commotion on the other side of the barricade. She looked and saw that the crane was gently setting the next casket on the back of a flatbed truck. She tugged Hank by the sleeve of his windbreaker, and they both headed over to join Coil and Jakes.

"Anyone want to make a guess?" Jakes asked.

"I'll guess it's the same thing as the last one," Agatha replied.

"Wow, you really like to go out on a limb, don't you?" Hank taunted her.

"Well," Agatha said. "If you look at it logically, I can see the same amount of strain on this one that was caused by the last one. Gold is heavy."

"Very observant," Hank mused.

"I'm always watching, big boy."

The FBI crime scene techs opened the lid and gave Jakes the affirmative, and Jakes radioed his second unit of SWAT operators who had been assigned to remain on site to escort the casket and contents back to their forensics lab.

The other SWAT team had radioed earlier that they'd safely delivered their package and were returning to Rusty Gun. It looked like they'd have the third casket up and open before midnight. It didn't make Agatha any less cold, but it did mean she'd be in bed before dawn.

"Let's get the last one going," Jakes said to the crew.

Agatha could see Jakes was exhausted. Things hadn't started smoothly with his arrival in Rusty Gun. But after he'd gotten back on equal footing with Hank, he'd really shown his skill at organizing the investigation.

Coil came over with boxes stacked two high. "Look what the Taco and Waffle sent over."

Agatha grabbed the top container and helped Coil hand out Styrofoam cups of piping hot tortilla soup. They all moved into a mobile command post that had been requisitioned by Coil to support their operation. It was like a luxury mobile home. Agatha snuck her cell phone out to take pictures of the interior. It was definitely going into a book.

The excavation of the fifth and final coffin would take about an hour, so sitting in a very cozy command center watching cable television wasn't the worst thing in the world.

Agatha was into her second episode of *Murder She Wrote* when Jakes pulled the exterior door open.

"Let's see if the third time is the charm," Jakes said.

Agatha moaned as she unfolded her aching body out of a comfortable chair. Sure, it was exciting to see those amounts of treasure, but to be honest, she'd already witnessed it twice. How much more exciting could a third casket get?

"You want to do the honors?" Jakes asked Agatha as he held his hand out to help her up and onto the flatbed transport truck.

"Umm, yeah," she said.

Agatha stood back as they jimmied open the lid and removed it. She slipped on her phone light and shined it into the coffin. It was empty.

"Well?" Jakes asked.

"It's empty," she said.

"I don't know if that's disappointing or our big break," Hank said.

"What do you mean?" Agatha asked, hopping down from the flatbed.

"Maybe Lawrence's outlier is actually the one who buried them here. When that much money is involved, there's no honor among thieves."

"I just got a text from Lawrence," Jakes said. "He says it's imperative that he speak with us about the third victim."

"Does that mean we get to go back inside?" Agatha asked.

"Yes."

"Then count me in." she said.

Jakes dialed up Lawrence on the computer screen in the command post. "Dr. Lawrence," Jakes said. "You don't have to put your face so close to the screen. We can see you just fine."

"Right," Lawrence said. "It seems my deductions were correct about the other victims. Number three is identified as Emma Gurtz. History has her as something of a rabble-rouser in her day. Was something of a Tom-boy, spent her time fishing and hunting with her brothers. And drinking in the bars. She'd been known to throw a punch or two, but her family was quite prominent and was able to keep the law off her. Found she had quite a talent at pouring drinks and lending an ear to those drinking her supplies.

"How'd her family get their money?" Agatha asked.

"I believe you call it Texas Tea," Lawrence said.

"Oil," Hank and Agatha said together, and shared a look.

"What about the contents of the coffin?" Coil asked.

"Jakes's boys have removed the contents and taken them into another area. They're still cataloguing the contents and getting an assessment on the dates and value of the gold and someone is coming in to appraise the diamonds. They did confirm it was Confederate gold that had probably been stolen by the militia in an attempt to launch a fight for Texas to regain their independence."

"Anything else?" Jakes asked.

"There was a cache of documents. They'll have to be sorted, but it looks like an accounting journal and deeds."

"Deeds?" Jakes asked.

"Yes, property and mineral rights mostly."

"Interesting," Jakes said. "Very interesting."

Chapter Twelve

THURSDAY

Agatha skipped out on her morning run. She'd slept fitfully the night before, her brain processing all the information she'd learned about the victims. She finally gave up on sleep and spent the last hours before sunrise in the war room, and she wasn't surprised to get the early morning text from Hank. They were a lot alike when their minds started clicking, and she wasn't surprised to find he'd spent a sleepless night as well.

She agreed to meet him and Coil for breakfast at the Kettle Café before the team briefing at the sheriff's office. Hank was already waiting at their usual table, but Coil wasn't there yet.

"Sleep good?" Hank asked.

"Nope," she said. "My mind was racing all night."

Hank held up three fingers when the waitress looked over. He'd already taken care of their drinks.

"Me either," he said. "I figured you were in the same boat. I keep thinking about the empty coffin. I wasn't surprised by it. If Lawrence is right about these five

60

women and their friendship and business partnership, then it makes sense to think the nun is the key to this whole mystery. She's the missing piece."

"I agree," Agatha said. "Sister Rosa Anita Immaculate was her ordained name, but I'm having trouble finding a given name. Maybe Lawrence was able to find something more on her, but my resources don't run as deep as his do."

"Looks like my timing is perfect," Lawrence said from behind Agatha.

She jumped in surprise when he scooted into the booth next to her, and she gave Hank an accusing stare. He could've warned her.

Lawrence looked terrible. He hadn't slept for the last forty-eight, and he was still dressed in the same canary-yellow shirt and tan trousers he'd worn the day before. And it was obvious he hadn't showered, combed his hair, or shaved.

"What are you doing here?" Hank asked. "I thought Jakes ordered you to submit a written report and get some sleep."

"This is too good not to share in person," he said, and then called out the waitress. "I need coffee. Black."

"How about you wait until everyone gets together for the briefing?" Hank suggested. "Jakes isn't going to be happy."

"I figured I'd relay it to you. I'm quite fond of this group. Jakes, not so much. Besides, I'm not sure how much longer I'm going to be able to stay awake, so this may be the only time I get to say it."

"Okay," Agatha said. "Let's hear it."

"Hear what?" Coil asked from behind her.

Agatha jumped. "Crud, is everybody going to sneak up on me today?"

"To be fair, they only snuck up on you because your

back was to the door," Hank said. "Good timing, Coil. Lawrence was just about to brief us."

"But, didn't Jakes…"

"Just sit down," Agatha said, unable to wait any longer. "Go ahead Lawrence. And maybe scoot over a little bit."

"I've discovered the identity of victim number four," he said. "And I was right. The exotic dancer. Ruth Anne Wilkerson was her name. But get this, she might have been dancing in the evenings and carousing with her girlfriends, but in the daytime, she was the administrative assistant to the superintendent of the Texas Rangers."

"What?" Coil asked, his eyes going wide. "I'm assuming they didn't know of her nighttime activities."

"Oh, I think some people knew. You don't work the underground without coming across a few people who live on the wealthy side of the tracks. But if they told her secret they'd also be exposing their own sins. Her family was well connected and wealthy, which was how she got the job."

"Let me guess," Hank said. "They're an oil family."

"Quite right," Lawrence said, his grin somewhat maniacal in his sleep deprived face. "It's quite unusual if you follow the paper trail. County deeds showed an expansive plot of acreage having been redesignated from agricultural to industrial in the early part of the century. A lot of people lost their land, and the Wilkerson's became one of the wealthiest families in the state when those oil rigs went up on their newly designated property."

"That gives other people a reason to hate the Wilkerson's," Hank said, "but it doesn't explain why Ruth Wilkerson was killed and buried in a false grave, or how millions of dollars in Confederate gold was buried with her."

"Well, it's not like these women were pillars of the community," Agatha said. "Their families had money, but that would only take them so far. They struck out on their own and chose a dangerous path. A bootlegger, a madam, the speakeasy owner, and the exotic dancer joined forces and made sinning easy for the people of San Antonio. They knew who was breaking the law, cheating on their wives, and drinking away their troubles. They'd have been very powerful in their own way in the underbelly of that city. And people would be afraid. Maybe they were also blackmailers."

"That's a good angle," Hank said. "Maybe some of the papers recovered can be salvaged."

Coil put a ten down on the table to cover the coffees and tip. "Time to get to the briefing. Lawrence, I'd make myself scarce. If you show up in that office Jakes is liable to shoot you."

"Excellent advice."

Chapter Thirteen

SPECIAL AGENT JAKES MONOPOLIZED MOST OF THE SPACE inside the conference room at the sheriff's office. Hank slipped in between the gaps of people and found an empty seat, and he waved for Agatha to join him.

Coil rolled a beat-up leather chair out of his office and settled into a corner across from Hank. They tended to situate themselves opposite from one another in social settings so they could communicate across the room.

Jakes ushered in the new batch of FBI agents who had been assigned to him. They were dressed in starched khaki tactical trousers and matching navy-blue polo shirts.

"Welcome everyone," Jakes began. "I've got a report from Dr. Andrew Lawrence detailing his latest findings. You should each have a copy."

Hank nudged Agatha with his elbow. She was frowning, and he could feel the tension in her. Jakes had been casual for the most part, but the arrival of extra agents had him upping the formality.

"Since Dr. Lawrence isn't here, take a moment to look

over the report, and I'll answer questions or relay them to Dr. Lawrence."

"No need," Lawrence said, pushing into the room like a hurricane. "I'm here."

Hank and Coil shared a look, and Coil just shook his head. For all his brilliance, Dr. Lawrence was a real dummy.

"What are you doing here?" Jakes demanded.

"Aren't I part of the team?" Lawrence asked with a dejected look on his face. "I created the document, so it's only fair that I explain it. Besides, I caught my second wind. Or maybe my third. I lost count."

"In the meantime," Jakes said. "Don't stand downwind, because I've smelled corpses that have a better odor than you right now."

"Well," Lawrence huffed. "That was rude."

"Run it down," Jakes barked. "Then I order you to go shower and sleep. In that order."

"I'm not sure you can order me," Lawrence said, looking perplexed, but when Jakes growled and took a step forward, Lawrence waved the comment away. "I've confirmed the identity of each of the four victims recovered, but finding cause of death is going to take considerably more time. I need to clean the bones and then study them, but there are interesting markings on victim two that could have come from a bullet. I'll swab and test the area.

"I've also spent a great deal of time looking at the documents. They're really in quite good shape. The ink is faded some, but technology will help us with that. What we initially thought were bank journals are actually gaming ledgers."

"Ahh," Hank said. "Now that makes sense."

"The ledgers ended not long after Prohibition did in

December nineteen thirty-three," Lawrence replied. "I guess they saw their enterprise going down the drain, but that didn't mean they hadn't amassed a lot of cash in the years prior. Whoever was holding onto the illegal earnings needed a place to hide the money before Elliot Ness and his infamous Untouchables seized it all. They were rounding people up left and right toward the end of Prohibition."

"Wasn't Elliot Ness busy chasing Al Capone?" Agatha asked.

"Capone was just one of many targets," Lawrence explained, "but the Bureau of Prohibition continued investigating and making arrests and seizures until nineteen forty-four."

Hank jumped a bit when Agatha pinched his triceps. She leaned into him and covered her mouth with a hand.

"I think this blows your theory that the Rattlers are involved in this," she said. "You're going to have to pay up."

It ain't over till it's over," Hank said.

"Are you whispering about me?" Lawrence asked, his look seething. "Everyone is being quite rude today. I'll not stand for it any longer."

"Despite what you might think," Hank said. "You are not the center of everyone's universe. So, feel free to keep going."

"Oh, then clearly you have a theory since the two of you are huddled together whispering." Lawrence took an aggressive step forward. "Please, delight us all with your brilliance."

"I actually do have a theory," Hank said. "But sharing it with you is not on my list of priorities, since the last time I checked, you weren't in charge of the case."

A crazy look came into Lawrence's eyes and he let out

an earsplitting shriek as he launched himself at Hank. Agatha just stared in wide-eyed horror as Lawrence's face ran right into Hank's fist. Lawrence dropped to the floor cold.

"Maybe he'll finally get some sleep," Hank said, rolling him over with the tip of his foot. "Best thing I could've done for him."

"Would've been nice if you could've sprayed him with the hose first," Coil said. "My carpet is going to smell terrible."

Chapter Fourteen

AGATHA SETTLED BACK IN THE PASSENGER'S SEAT AS HANK
steered them toward Fredericksburg. She enjoyed the ride.
Lately, they hadn't had much time alone to just talk. Hank
always seemed to be more open to sharing how he felt
when they drove. It was something about not having the
eye to eye that allowed him to talk freely.

"You sure the Gurtz's are going to meet with us?"
Agatha asked.

"That's what Coil said. Apparently, they're as curious
about their family history as we are, especially now that
Emma's remains have been recovered."

"I'm sure it's hard to find closure when there's no
body," Hank said. "But I wonder how receptive they're
going to be when we start asking questions about the
family fortune?"

"We'll play that one by ear," she said, and then closed
her eyes to listen to the rest of her audiobook.

"What are you listening to?" Hank asked.

"A book."

"What book?" he asked.

She sighed and took out her earbuds. "No book, because you won't stop interrupting me."

"Must be good," Hank said, his mouth quirking at the growl in her throat.

"It is. Or it would be if you'd be quiet. Addison is just about to get into trouble."

"Addison Holmes?" he asked. "By Liliana Hart?"

"You read her, too?" she asked.

"I love her J.J. Graves Mystery Series. It's on the money, and you know how hard I am about my police procedural novels. I've read all her books."

"Must be nice," she said pointedly, and put her earbuds back in.

It wasn't long before Hank slowed and turned into Golden Vistas Winery. The stone pillars and ornate iron gates were reminiscent of Tuscany, and the looming bed and breakfast was inviting.

"Beautiful," Agatha said. "I can only imagine what it looks like when the vineyards are green and ripe with grapes. We're past the season."

They were met by an attendant who directed them to the south side of the property where there was a well-kept villa that was much smaller than the main house. An elderly woman waited outside to greet them. Her smile looked strained, but it wasn't unfriendly.

"Ms. Gurtz?" Agatha asked as they got out of the car.

"It's Gurtz-Shepherd now," she said. "I'm guessing y'all are from the sheriff's office?" She looked to be in her mid to late sixties. Her hair was white and hung in soft curls to her shoulders, her face was unashamedly weathered from her time spent in the sun, and she wore bright red lipstick.

"Yes, ma'am," Agatha said. "I'm Agatha Harley, and this is my partner, Hank Davidson."

Hank nodded. "Thank you for seeing us, ma'am."

"Oh, you don't have to ma'am me to death," she said, smiling. "Just call me Emmy. Everyone does. I was named after her, you know."

"No, ma'am," Agatha said. "I mean, Emmy."

"Y'all come on inside. There's a chill in the air today."

The office interior was purposefully rustic—exposed beams, square-head nails, and hand-scraped wooden floors.

"We'd given up hope of ever knowing what really happened to Emma," Emmy said, taking a seat in a comfortable looking leather chair. She directed them to the matching couch across from her and they sat.

"Why's that?" Agatha asked.

"You know how families are?" Emmy said. "Emma was the talk of the town back in the day, and even after the day if you know what I mean. Until she wasn't. There was always talk about her. A woman as colorful as Emma was bound to cause talk, good and bad. But she was ours, and we're grateful to her. Everything we have is because of her."

"I understand," Hank said. "We don't have a cause of death, but extenuating circumstances surrounding how her body was discovered lead us to believe she didn't die of natural causes."

"Of course not," Emmy said. "Girl disappears in her early twenties, never to be heard from again. She's either living the high life or she's dead. No bones about it. I'm just glad we can put her to rest and give her a proper burial."

"You said everything you have is because of her," Agatha said. "She gave you this property?"

Emmy nodded. "It wasn't always a vineyard. It started out as a field of oil derricks, but oil derricks don't bring in tourism. It turns out the soil here is good for growing grapes, so here we are."

"But Texas is oil country," Agatha said.

"You still have oil being drilled," Hank said.

"You bet," she said. "And it's going to keep drilling until the ground runs dry. It's hard to see unless you look, and most of the tourist only see the acres of vineyards."

"So how did Emma contribute to the legacy?" Agatha asked.

"All I know is what was passed down in our family, but you know how things get distorted, so who knows. We were always told she came here from San Antonio with a stack of property deeds that had all been transferred into her name. It was nothing to get your drilling permits stamped back then. No EPA breathing down your neck. Emma signed all the deeds to a family trust she had some lawyer friend create and named her parents as the executors. When she disappeared and there was no sign of her for several years, she was declared legally dead and her parents took control."

"How did Emma get the deeds?" Hank asked.

"Said she won them in a card game," Emmy said, shrugging. "Made sense to me, considering the kind of life she lived and the people she hung out with."

"We did a little research on this land, and that's the part we can't figure out," Hank said. Before she ended up with the deeds, this stretch of land was owned by seven different land owners, and they all signed their property over to Emma without any bill of sale."

Emmy's mouth pursed tightly, and Agatha could tell she didn't like the direction this was going. But the reality was, all of the Gurtz property had been stolen, and the original owners had been put out on their cans after Emma ended up with their property.

Emma stood and walked to the door, holding it open for them. "I have no idea why people would gamble everything they have away, but they do it every day. Nothing much has changed there. I appreciate y'all coming out. Please let me know when her remains can be taken for burial."

"Yes, ma'am," Agatha said.

"May I ask you one question before we start back on our long drive?" Hank asked.

"You can, but I can't promise I'll answer."

"Fair enough," he said. "Where is Mr. Shepherd? You did say your name was Gurtz-Shepherd?"

"We're divorced," she said, and closed the door in their faces.

They were in the car driving away before Agatha asked why he'd wanted to know that.

"This is a small community," he said. "Even smaller back in the twenties and thirties, and the families who got their land stolen would have had to go somewhere. But chances are they didn't go far. People just didn't live outside of what was familiar to them back then. So, you have to imagine the people around here would be a bit resentful that one family has owned all of this for all this time, when the seven other families know it should've been theirs. Emmy has stories passed down from her family, you'd better believe the other seven have stories that have been passed down too."

"I guess you're right, but what does Shepherd have to do with this, and why now?"

"She said her name was Gurtz-Shepherd," Hank said. "The hyphen wasn't used back then, so why would she continue to use her ex-husband's name?"

"How'd you know she was divorced?" Agatha asked.

He shrugged. "Traditional woman, but she wore no ring on her left hand. There was a small ring on her right hand that looked like a family heirloom, so she wasn't averse to wearing jewelry. There wasn't even a tan line or an indentation to show she'd worn a wedding band anytime recently.

"If you noticed, the pictures in her office were only her and two adult daughters. There was no husband in any of them."

"Good point," Agatha said.

"It was mostly just to rile her up," Hank said with a chuckle. "I do not appreciate being kicked out like that. Especially when you could see she knew exactly what Emma had done to those people."

"Now what?" she asked

"Now we go visit Mr. Shepherd. Because I bet he's willing to tell the whole story."

"Very impressive," she said. "How about I track him down?"

"How about it," Hank said.

A few minutes passed before Agatha said, "He's not but a couple of miles from us." And then she gave him the address.

Hank turned into the long driveway of a modest ranch called Circle S. A young man shot baskets in front of the garage. Hank parked the car and then introduced himself to the young man, showing him his badge. The young man ran inside, and it wasn't too long before a man in his sixties came out the front door. He was beanpole thin and as tall as Hank, and his silver hair was full and luxurious. His belt buckle was so big, Agatha wondered how he was able to stand upright.

"Mr. Shepherd?" Hank asked.

"That's me. You the police?"

"Yes, sir," Hank said, showing his badge again.

Mr. Shepherd nodded. "Young William told me you were here to ask questions about the Gurtz winery." And then he broke out into a grin. "Boy, have I got a story for you."

Chapter Fifteen

FRIDAY

Agatha made sure to wrap up before she left the house to head to the café. The days were getting cold enough that she'd dug out the North Face jacket she'd bought to go snow skiing several years before. The jacket was the only good thing to come out of that adventure.

A realtor was coming by later to look at her home. It was time. She still wasn't a hundred percent sure about selling it, but she'd never know for sure unless she dipped her toe in the water. Maybe November wasn't even a good month for listing a house, but who knew?

She hadn't talked to Hank about it, but she didn't want to say anything until she was completely sure she was going to sell it. Hank had talked about her moving in with him, but it hadn't been brought up since the month before. And to be honest, she really wasn't in favor of shacking up. She was still very much an old-fashioned girl, and living together wasn't something she saw in her future.

She got to the café first and thought about her choices as she drank her first cup of coffee. She flipped through the emails that cluttered her inbox until she came upon one from her literary agent. Agatha had only been answering things that had been time sensitive or absolutely necessary, and she felt guilty about it because her agent was a good woman. The email headline read, *Hollywood here we come*! She just wasn't as excited about things as her agent was.

"Mind if I sit?"

The voice startled her, and Agatha looked up. It was Jakes.

"Sorry," she said. "I was lost in work emails. Please, sit."

She looked to see if the others were behind him, but he was alone. He was so tall he had trouble wedging himself in the booth across from her, and he ended up sitting at an angle with his long legs propped up so he could see her and the door.

"I want to apologize to you," Jakes said.

"For what?" she asked, surprised.

"He's coming back," Jakes said somberly.

Her heart stuttered in her chest, and she felt the air leave the room as fear took over. "Salt?" she asked, her voice weak.

"Who?" Jakes asked, confused, and then the lightbulb clicked. "Oh, no," he assured her. "You made sure he's never coming back. I didn't mean to scare you."

She let out a shuddering breath as her lungs started working again.

"I meant Lawrence," he said. "I know he's been bothering you. Hank told me y'all have a history."

"We were engaged," Agatha said. "And Lawrence is at best an annoyance. But he's brilliant at his job. Besides, I've got Hank, and Hank has a mean right hook."

Jakes laughed. "Yes, he does. He clocked him cold. We got Lawrence settled in at the motel and let him sleep it off for about twenty hours. So, he's fresh and back on duty. I just wanted to give you the heads up."

"I appreciate it," she said. "But I'm good."

"Hank's a great guy," Jakes said. "A good cop and a good friend. He looks happy around you. I'm glad for it."

Agatha knew Jakes connection to Hank's wife being murdered, and she could appreciate the emotional past they had together.

"I'm glad for it too," she said.

"There room for two more?" Hank asked, coming up to the table.

"No, but we could move to a table," Jakes said, pointing toward the front of the café.

They all shuffled to the new table and the waitress brought their drinks and menus.

"I hear the two of you had a very interesting conversation last night," Coil said once they'd ordered.

"That we did," she said. "Mr. Shepherd had been waiting to unload for years, but there was never anyone willing to listen to him."

"Think it was legit?" Jakes asked.

"As accurate as memory can be," Agatha said. "But fortunately, he had the written records. In a nutshell, Fredericksburg in the twenties was nothing more than hard land to farm. The area wasn't optimum for plowing, and although the Great Depression was still a few years away, the town lived in a state of economic turmoil."

"Shepherd said they were so poor that no one in the town knew there was a depression going on in the rest of the world," Hank added.

"Apparently the Gurtz family—that would be Emma's parents—had oil men sent by the church scouting everyone's property on the sly. They discovered oil across that huge swatch of land, and that's when the plan started to form. Emma Gurtz began to swindle everyone into signing over their mineral rights."

"Why would anyone agree to that?" Coil asked.

"They didn't at first," Agatha said. "But then things got aggressive. Livestock started being slaughtered, then a family pet or two. Then one of the farm houses burned to the ground with a family of five inside. None of them made it out, and neighbors described the fire as having started everywhere at once. People were scared and they eventually did what they were told."

"The key is in that empty coffin," Jakes said.

"Bingo," Hank said, touching his nose. "And I think we're going to need Lawrence if we're going to figure it out."

Chapter Sixteen

"Jakes mentioned you brought up Salt," Hank said a little later as they were walking back to the sheriff's office. The others had gone on ahead, so it was just the two of them.

"Yeah," she said. "It was weird. I didn't mean to. I just had other things on my mind, and he was the first thing I thought of."

"That doesn't sound good."

"No, I think it answered a question for me," she said. "I'm going to sell my house. For sure. I called a realtor and she's coming out today."

He was silent for a couple of minutes. "You know you're welcome to stay with me, until…"

"Until I find a place of my own?" Agatha said.

"That's not it," he said, drawing her closer. "I don't think you're the live-in type. I'm not either. We're more… permanent kind of people."

She waited to hear what she wanted him to say, but the words didn't come. She shook her head and took his hand.

Hopefully, he could learn to say the words sometime before she moved into a nursing home.

"Come on," she said. "We'll be late."

They were, but the others, including Lawrence were waiting on them. Lawrence was sporting one heck of a shiner, but he was showered and shaved, and he was back in one of his expensive suits, this one charcoal gray.

"Before we start," he said. "I'd like to apologize. My behavior was inappropriate. I promise it'll be all business from this point forward. Now, to business. We've discovered that Ruth Anne Wilkerson was indeed the personal secretary to the Texas Rangers superintendent," Lawrence said. "She was an exemplary employee, as was reflected in her quarterly evaluations. But she was young, and that was how they tempted her."

"Who is they?" Hank asked.

"I'm not sure," Lawrence replied. "There are no recorded intelligence reports of mafia activity or enterprise in the area. I don't believe it was mob related at all, despite similar circumstances happening in some of the bigger crime cities.

"The Rangers' investigation showed that she first violated their integrity and morality code of conduct when a photograph of her surfaced while she was doing one of her dances. She became the weak link in the chain. Once the Rangers got hold of the photograph and saw the illegal activities taking place in the background, they began an undercover sting operation into her activities, and soon discovered straw-man assets that included…"

"Let me guess," Agatha said. "Oil and mineral rights."

"Yes," he said. "But they were all legal transactions, so there was nothing the Rangers could do except fire her for violating their morality clause. Records showed that, following her termination, police raids began to target speakeasies throughout San Antonio. One report that was classified, and a little tricky to get my hands on, detailed that Elliot Ness himself was coordinating a visit to Texas," Lawrence said. "Although it didn't say specifically where he was going to raid, the report referred to San Antonio and the Nun."

"Back to the nun," Hank said. The Nun is who was supposed to be in that fifth casket."

"Any of those police reports about the raids mention a nun or church or anything like that?" Jakes asked.

"Not yet," Lawrence replied.

"Was Ruth Anne ever arrested in one of those raids?" Coil asked.

"Good question," Agatha said. "But why haven't we been asking the bigger question?

The room went silent.

"Which is?" Lawrence asked.

"Who made off with the contents from the first two coffins?"

"What makes you think there was contents taken from the first two coffins?" Jakes asked.

"Why wouldn't there be?" Agatha replied.

"I think that's being a bit presumptuous," Jakes said.

"I think it's absolutely reasonable."

"Don't you think we're busy working on that?" Jakes snapped, his frustration clear.

"I didn't mean to imply that you weren't," she said, "but it's never come up in these briefings."

"That would be my error," he said. "We've split the case into two separate investigations. Because of your knowledge and connection to the locals, you've been allowed to participate in identifying the remains, while other field agents are tracking down the thefts."

"Allowed?" she said under her breath, her brows raising.

Hank nudged her with his elbow. She knew she had no official authority, but there was no reason to be a jerk.

"So, what's the progress on the missing coffins?" she asked

"Classified," Jakes replied. "We're dismissed." And with that, he turned on his heel and walked out.

Agatha and Hank remained in the conference room as the others went about their duties. She didn't want to talk inside, so she tugged Hank's hand so he'd follow. They walked across Main Street and she ran her arm through Hank's arm as she led him window shopping along the strip.

"You want to tell me what's going on?" he asked.

"Hank, I've got a bad feeling. Something's not right. It's been days and there's not been a peep about the first two caskets. Somebody walked away with millions in diamonds and gold, and the lead investigator is camped out here like it's going to fall into his lap instead of actually investigating."

Hank pulled her into his arms and held her close.

"Hank?" she asked.

"Since we're being watched, we might as well give them something to talk about," he said.

"Watched?" she asked. "By who, the Feds?"

"Dot Williams," he said, chuckling.

"Stop that, I'm being serious."

"I figured everyone works a case in their own way," Hank explained. "I wasn't going to ask because we'd been so active in tracking down the families of the deceased. But his reaction to your questions made me realize that we've been given busy work to keep us away from the real investigation."

"You saw Coil's reaction," she said. "He knows more than he's shared. And there's something else that struck me as odd earlier in the café."

"Besides the eggs?"

"I'm being serious."

"Sorry," he said.

"When Jakes and I were talking he started the conversation by apologizing and saying *he* was coming back. I said, Salt? And Jakes knew who I was talking about. How and why would he know about Salt?"

"Good question," he said, squeezing her arm in warning not to say too much. "Good question.

Chapter Seventeen

Hank heard the knock on Agatha's front door, but she was sprawled out on the chaise and looked like she had no plans to go anywhere. Hank waved at her to relax and went to answer the door.

"Heard Agatha had come home sick," Coil said. "Thought I'd stop in and check on her."

"She's in the war room," Hank said.

They walked back through the house, and Hank had been right. Agatha hadn't moved a muscle.

"Hey, Agatha," Coil said. "Feeling okay?"

"Not really," she said.

"Think you caught a bug?" he asked. "I can call Shelly to bring over some comfort food."

"You know what would make me feel a whole lot better?" she asked.

"What's that?"

"The truth."

Hank had moved across the room so he could watch Coil's reaction. The man never flinched.

"Truth about what?"

"We've been friends a long time," Hank said. "Now isn't the time to start trying to be a good liar."

"I'm an excellent liar," Coil said. "I worked undercover."

"You're only an excellent liar to people who don't know you inside and out."

Coil blew out a breath. "It's complicated, and my hands are tied."

"No problem," Agatha said. "Thanks for stopping by."

"Come on y'all. Don't act this way. You know I'm an open book on cases, but this is out of my hands."

"I said we understand," she said. "But there's no reason for you to be here. Hank and I have been jerked around in this thing from the start. We're kicked off the scene, and then all of a sudden, we're essential to the team. Which is bull, because all we're good for is running around like chickens with their heads cut off doing busy work and gathering details. I'm not a fan of being used by anyone."

Coil looked at Hank.

"Don't look at me," Hank said. "She's right, and you know it. There's no reason for you to be here right now."

Coil's face tightened and Agatha could see the war raging there. But ultimately, he decided to nod stiffly and walk out the door. She locked it behind him.

"How about a motorcycle ride?" Hank asked.

"What? Now?"

"I'm going with my gut. I'm going to grab my bike. Be ready when I get back."

"Go where?"

"Just be ready," he said.

It wasn't twenty minutes before Hank rolled back in front of Agatha's house on his big Harley. The November sun was bright, but it was still leather wearing weather. He smiled as Agatha rushed out the door. He loved seeing her in the all black leather outfit.

"Where are we going?" she demanded.

"We need a little wind therapy to clear our heads."

Hank knew it was time to color outside the lines. It wasn't like he was still working with the FBI. And he was only a volunteer detective for Coil. There was nothing that said he couldn't get on his bike and take a ride.

He throttled it wide open at the Waco exit sign and leaned back until he felt the connection with Agatha. That was the joy of the open road, and he loved sharing it with her.

Half an hour later they rolled into the parking lot of Reverend Graham's Harley Davidson store. Hank rode back toward the service section. As expected, there was Sully.

"Hank?" Sully said, once Hank had cut the engine. "That you?"

Hank lifted the tinted shield on his full-faced helmet to show Sully it was him.

"Hey, man," Hank said. "Can you take a look at my bike? I think I lost something along the road back near a cemetery."

Sully shook his head and came toward him. "Rookie."

Hank towered over the five-foot seven-inch biker. Sully's long, salt and pepper matted hair was held back by a black bandana, and a Houston Astro's baseball cap.

"I'll look at it," Sully said as he nodded to Agatha and knelt next to the v-twin engine.

Agatha climbed off the other side and walked into the store to watch out for anyone paying too much attention to Hank and Sully.

"Have any idea what's missing?" Hank whispered.

Sully stiffened, but there was no mistaking that he

understood Hank was talking about the coffins and not the bike. "I think I can help you out with this," Sully said, fiddling with the kickstand.

Agatha loses. His gut had said from the beginning that the Rattlers were involved.

"Really?" he asked.

"It's complicated," Sully said, continuing to whisper. "I could lose my job permanently, if you know what I mean." He swiped a finger across his throat.

"Can we talk here?" Hank asked.

"Tonight would be better."

That was too big of a risk. Hank might've jeopardized Sully's life just by showing up, but they could pass this meeting off. Going away and coming back would definitely bring suspicion and unwanted attention for both of them.

"Old buddy," Hank said, moving in close. "I really need to know now."

Sully's weathered face looked like it had been set on fire and extinguished with a barbed wire baseball bat. He'd lived a rough life along America's highways and back alleys. And it showed. But the expression of dread carved deep into the outlaw twisted Hank's gut.

Sully nodded and then scribbled something onto an old receipt and handed it to Hank.

"What's this?" Hank asked.

"My sister's number," Sully said. "She's down in Laredo. You know, just in case."

"Will do, my friend," Hank said.

"Ever heard of Elliot Ness?" Sully asked.

Hank was caught off guard by the question, but he nodded.

"There was an old syndicate back in the day, when the government outlawed booze."

"During Prohibition?" Hank asked.

"Yep, that's the word," Sully said. "This syndicate ran most of the moonshine operations across Texas. They were unstoppable. Rattler history says we entered into a deal with them."

"Y'all have history books?"

"Yeah, goes back a couple hundred years," Sully said.

"So, the Rattlers were in bed with the mafia during Prohibition?" Hank asked, just so he was clear.

But Sully just chuckled. "There wasn't no mafia in Texas, son. Them speakeasies were run by The Church."

"The church?" Hank asked.

"Yes, siree," said Sully.

"What's Elliot Ness have to do with a church?"

"Not a church," Sully said. "The Church.".

"What religion is the church?" agitated, Hank pressed.

Sully wheezed out a laugh. "The church of what feels good now."

"Can we get serious?" Hank asked. "Look, the police know you were in the area of that cemetery, so if you want me to help you, you have to lay it out for me."

Sully stood up and limped away from Hank.

"I had nothing to do with them cats getting smoked," Sully said.

It was everything Hank could do to not let the surprise show on his face. He could've strangled Jakes. If Sully was talking murder, then Jakes had really left them in the dark.

"You need to play straight with me," Hank told him. "You think the FBI won't throw you under the bus for a couple of murders just to see the case closed?

"Fine," Sully said. "But I'm starting to think retirement on a tropical island is starting to sound pretty good."

"I'll come visit," Hank said. "Now tell me."

"The Church was a crime syndicate during the

twenties. They weren't around for long, but they were very powerful. And evil. Their head honcho was a nun."

"You remember her name?" Hank asked.

"Everyone just called her Sister Rosa."

"Sister Rosa Anita Immaculate?" Hank asked.

"That sounds right. She ran the church's finances for years, then eventually skimmed enough to go out on her own. She created The Church, and her and a few of her friends built an underground empire."

"Were the other four girls nuns?" Hank asked.

"I don't think so, but that's how they dressed when they were hauling white lightning. Everyone knew, even the local police, but they'd been bought off, so they looked the other way."

"What happened?" Hank asked.

"One of them got busted."

"The one who worked for the Texas Rangers?"

"Yep," he said. "That was real smart to have an insider in there. The Rangers worked a lot of Prohibition busts, and she'd have known when and where they were planning to raid. But she was found out, and they started following her. Word was, Elliot Ness was coming down himself to raid The Church's underground headquarters just outside of San Antonio."

"There was never a raid," Hank said. "Not that we can find. What happened?"

Sully swallowed. "The nun hired the Rattlers to help her clean house.

"What else do you know?" Hank looked around at the increased people milling around.

"I know that the Nun hired the Rattlers to help her do a little house cleaning."

"Your history books have all the details?" Hank asked.

"A lot of people would like to see into our archives," he

said, waggling his eyebrows. "The Nun shot her four partners and buried them in caskets filled with a fortune. And then she hired the Rattlers to dig the five graves and bury the bodies of her friends. Of course, we didn't know about all the treasure inside. Thought it was just the bodies. But word is the caskets were real nice, expensive, and sealed well. Gotta figure that kind of casket is protecting something valuable."

"Why dig five graves?" Hank asked. "The fifth casket we dug up was empty."

"The Nun said that the empty coffin was a sign to anyone who tried to rob her. She'd bury them in there herself. My Rattler brothers who'd dug the graves were getting suspicious at that point, and they planned to go back and dig up the graves."

"Why didn't they?"

"Because she shot and killed the only ones who knew where the treasure was buried. We've been looking for it ever since," he said, grinning.

"How come Sister Rosa never came back and reclaimed her gold?" Hank asked.

"Rumor was that while she was hiding from the law, she came across a church on the other side of the border. She apparently found God and took a vow of poverty to atone for all the wrongs she'd done.

"Wow," Hank said. "So how did you guys finally figure out where the treasure was buried after all this time? And why'd the Rattlers only dig up two of the graves?

Sully scoffed. "The Rattlers didn't steal that money. The Feds did."

Chapter Eighteen

HANK SPED THROUGH TOWN. HE WASN'T WORRIED whether Coil saw him or not. Agatha hadn't said a word since the conversation with Sully, but he knew she was processing everything she'd heard. They needed to get back to war room and see if they could substantiate any of the Rattler's history.

"Do you think Sully was telling the truth? Agatha asked.

"Yes."

"Wow, that seems definitive."

"Aggie, he knows stuff we just found out yesterday."

"What do you think about his Elliot Ness story?"

"It matches," Hank said. "There was a lot of money going around back then. How about some tacos? I'm starving."

"Now?" she asked.

Poor Agatha. She looked like she was about to explode. She'd been railroaded all week by an FBI special agent she wasn't sure she could trust, her former fiancé was in town,

Coil had been lying to her, her life was in turmoil over the adoption, and she was putting her house up for sale.

"Just trust me," Hank said.

"Fine," she said, throwing up her hands. "Let's go get tacos."

THE TACO AND WAFFLE WAS AS EXPECTED, VERY BUSY. That was exactly what Hank was hoping for. Secret surveillance microphones didn't record well in loud places, and while he wasn't sure Agatha's place had been bugged, it was better to be safe, and enjoy their tacos.

"Would you look at that," Agatha said, pointing to the wall behind the checkout counter. "Karl said they asked him about it."

It was a beautifully framed picture of Karl's momma, Sheila Johnson. Her murder had shaken the entire town. Her restaurant, Bucky's Brisket Basket, would never reopen, so since the Taco and Waffle had readjusted their work schedules to accommodate the extra customers, they also wanted to pay homage to a wonderful woman and citizen of Rusty Gun.

"That's a really kind gesture," he said, emotions clogging his throat. Sheila had been a good friend.

They were seated along a wall that looked out toward the sheriff's office. It seemed vacant, but Hank knew they were in there.

"Hank," Agatha said. "I think I've been very patient. But you're acting weird and you're kind of freaking me out."

"Yeah, I'm a little freaked out too," he said.

The waitress came and delivered their drinks, and he

waited until she'd gone away again before he started talking.

"Okay, so far we know that two coffins worth of gold are on the loose. We also know that the women's remains and the treasure all belonged to the crime organization called The Church, which was run by the Nun."

"This sounds like a movie," Agatha said.

"Right before we left Sully, he told me a couple of bodies were discovered out in a field and that's why Jakes and the Feds were in the area. Turns out the two bodies were his guys and they kept it hush hush. Jakes is in this neck deep. He had his guys steal the first two caskets and then ambushed them."

"How can that be?" she asked. "There hasn't been a peep about murdered cops. And how does Lawrence fit into this."

"This is what we like to call a cover up," Hank said. "Jakes told me Lawrence just showed up at the FBI Field Office while he was on sabbatical, looking for cases he could help with, and he just so happened to get assigned to Jakes."

"Really?" Agatha asked. "Because Lawrence told me Jakes specifically requested he come be part of a specialized unit. He never mentioned he was on sabbatical or anything other than where he'd been assigned."

"Jakes has always looked for cases that would make him a household name. If he'd found references to The Church in FBI files or even a geographic area of where the treasure might be hidden, he'd have jumped at the chance to solve it, and he wouldn't care who got in his way."

"You really think he stole the money?" she asked.

"I asked Lawrence about the other two caskets. He said he was given the remains and documents, but he said he never saw the rest of the contents again. They removed it to a secured location, and any time he asks he gets told to work in his assigned area. Lawrence said he didn't know where they moved the treasure, but he said it's not anywhere in the lab."

"What about Coil?" she asked nervously.

"He's into something, but I'm not even ready to consider he's in cahoots with Jakes."

"So, you're pretty sure Jakes is behind all of this?" she asked.

"It's looking that way," Hank said as he gazed back through the window toward Coil's office. "I let them misdirect me once, but it won't happen again."

"What's your gut on Sully and the Rattlers?"

Hank exhaled. He pulled the crumpled piece of paper out of his pocket and stared at it for a bit.

"I know he's on the up and up, but I can't figure out why he would've been in the area. It wasn't by coincidence. I think the Rattlers have a long memory to go along with their long history. If any one of them had caught wind of that money being recovered, I'm sure they'd want a piece of the pie as retribution for the brothers murdered by the Nun."

"Where do you think she put their bodies?" Agatha asked.

"It was a wilderness before a cemetery. I'm sure they made for animal snacks until there was nothing left."

"Do you think the fake names on the tomb stones meant anything? They seemed like a code?"

"My guess is they were just all part of the Nun's misinformation campaign. She was obviously brilliant, as well as brutal. Besides, who would ever think of messing with a nun?"

"So, what are we going to do?"

"It's time to back Coil into a corner."

Chapter Nineteen

"How deep are you?" Hank asked a little while later.

They'd met on the other side of town at an abandoned farmhouse where they used to go shooting. There was no one for miles around, and no one to hear if things went south.

Coil looked nervous. His eyes had dark circles beneath them, and his cheeks were more gaunt than usual.

Coil sighed. "Deep."

Hank's gut knotted and he felt the blood pound in his temples. "How deep?" He didn't bother to disguise the anger in his voice.

"I can't go into this, Hank," Coil said. "We've been here before, and you've got to trust me."

"Are you kidding? We're talking about the murder of federal agents. Friendship only goes so far."

Coil padded back and forth next to the farmhouse, his breathing shallow. Coil turned fast to face Hank, and Hank pulled his weapon, aiming it straight at center mass.

"Don't make any sudden moves," Hank said.

"What the heck are you doing?" Coil yelled.

"You're involved in the murder of federal agents, and the theft of millions of dollars as part of a corruption scheme with Jakes," Hank said.

"You've got it right, but not completely right."

"You've jerked Aggie and me around like two idiots while you and your partner steal millions beneath our noses. Was it your idea to throw Lawrence into the mix to provide a few laughs?"

"Dang it, Hank. Put that gun away."

Coil was sweating. He'd left his Stetson in his truck, and Hank could see the moist mop of hair that clung to his temples. Hank knew what Coil was capable of, and the good old boy routine was a diversion. Coil was deadly as a snake.

Coil put his hands up slowly. "What is it you really want?"

"I want the truth."

"I told you what I could," Coil said. "The smart thing would be to leave it at that. Put the gun away so we can talk."

"No thanks, I'd rather be safe."

"Safe from what?" Coil asked.

"I'll do to you what I've done to every killer I've encountered," Hank said. "I'll take you in, or I'll take you out. The choice is yours."

"Why can't you trust me for once?" Coil asked, desperation in his voice.

"I've trusted you since the moment we met. I would've died for you because that's how much I loved you. But you're asking me to throw away everything I've ever stood for, everything I am, and look the other way when you're in the wrong. And even worse, you've dragged Agatha into this mess. You're asking me to trust you, but how about you trust me with the truth. I've never betrayed you like this."

They stood at a standstill for several minutes. It seemed like an eternity. Hank finally sighed and holstered his pistol. He'd had enough. Coil left him no choice. He'd take Agatha out of Rusty Gun and contact Ranger Will Ellis with all of the facts. He'd let law enforcement deal with cleaning up the mess. Even if it meant his friend got swept up with it.

"Go do what you have to do," Hank said as he turned his back to walk to his car.

"Hank, stop."

Hank kept walking.

"Hank, don't make me do this," Coil called out.

"The choice is all yours," Hank said, and he walked on.

"Okay, fine. Fine! Here it is."

Hank stopped walking.

"I am involved, but not how you think. I'm investigating Jakes."

"What?" Hank asked.

"I'm working with the Texas Rangers," Coil said.

"How'd you get involved?"

"Some of the Rattlers were screwing around in the cemetery a few weeks ago, around the Alamo war heroes plot. The Rangers have an undercover agent in the Rattlers. The UC was able to take screenshots of the Rattler archives. It's incredible the history they've collected."

"I'm familiar with their history and the Church," Hank said.

"Figures," Coil said. "Unfortunately, we also think there's an FBI UC somewhere in the Rattlers hierarchy. It became a race to the finish to see who could dig up the caskets first. The Feds won. Whitehorse contacted me as soon as there was activity in the area so I could keep a watch out."

"What the Feds didn't know was that the Rangers had the whole cemetery under surveillance. They watched a very skilled crew of men arrive in the night to unearth the first two caskets. They emptied the contents but looked like they got spooked when motorcycles kept passing back and forth along the highway. Whitehorse's men followed the flatbed trucks until the ambush struck out in hill country."

"The Rattlers?" Hank guessed, but he knew better than to say anything he wasn't sure of.

"The men in the graveyard were a team of FBI contracted archeologists assigned to recover the bodies and the treasure. It was actually Dr. Lawrence who had discovered the burial location through his own independent research."

"Jakes had gotten pushed aside once Lawrence and the archaeologist came in, and he was pissed, so his team set up an ambush and killed them."

"Now no one knows where he took the contents?"

"Not at first, but Whitehorse was watching and waiting when the other caskets were recovered. Whitehorse reached out to me and as soon as there was a whisper the Rattlers and the FBI were about to set up shop in Rusty Gun, and he set a plan in motion. He wanted y'all involved but not in danger. I kept watch on Jakes in town, and the Rangers followed anyone that went anywhere beyond."

"What about Lawrence?"

"He's clean," Coil said. "And very lucky to be alive."

"What's the next move?" Hank asked.

"Yours is to go home and not say a word to Agatha. We've got too many moving parts and too many dangerous people with weapons. Now's not the time for heroes."

"I want to be a part of the takedown."

"Why, so you can get payback for Jakes's role in how Tammy died? There's no other reason on this earth for you to get involved in his arrest. I'm sorry, but this is out of my hands, and yours."

"I'm sure Whitehorse could use another seasoned detective," Hank said.

"Don't interfere, Hank," Coil said, putting a hand on his arm. Jason's already got a lot on his mind."

Hank looked at his screen and saw Agatha's message. His blood ran cold.

"Jakes is at Agatha's house," Hank said.

"What?" Coil asked. "I'm going to call Whitehorse to redirect manpower."

They sprinted to their respective vehicles and tore out down the dusty farm road. Hank called Agatha.

"What's going on?" he asked, relieved she'd answered.

"He's still at the door," she said. "I just had a bad feeling when he showed up, and I didn't answer."

"Good girl," he said. "Are you armed?"

"I am now," Agatha said.

"Don't let him in," Hank said. "Jakes is the killer. Coil and Whitehorse have been investigating him. If he steps foot inside your home, do not hesitate to shoot him."

"Got it," she said.

"The cavalry is on the way." Hank could hear Jakes calling her through the door. He was banging on it and demanding to be let inside. Hank's vision was narrowing as his heart raced with fury.

"I really can't wait to sell this house," she said.

Hank hadn't expected to laugh. "We'll be there soon, honey."

"He's pushing against the door," she said, sounding worried. "I think he's going to break it down."

"You know you don't have to wait until he enters the house to shoot him."

"I've got a better idea," Agatha said.

She went silent for a few moments. His heart was pounding out of his chest. He didn't want to yell into the phone in case it would give away her position. He tried to focus on the road, but once Coil had flown past traffic, the cars that had pulled over were pulling back onto the road and right in front of him. If only he had lights and a siren.

"Agatha?" he spoke softly into the BMW's microphone.

"I'm here."

"What's your better idea?"

"I slipped out the back door," she said. "I grew up here, and I know every nook and cranny in the neighborhood. Let him roam around the house looking for me. He'll be easier for y'all to find."

Hank let out another breath. "Smart. Very smart."

"But hurry. These bushes are scratching the dickins out of me."

Chapter Twenty

When Hank pulled across the front yard, Agatha's home was already surrounded by Texas Rangers. Sergeant Jason Whitehorse was walking Jakes out of Agatha's house. Jakes was cuffed, but his sheer bulk looked like he could snap the metal restraints in two at any moment.

Agatha was standing off to the side with Will Ellis, another friend and Texas Ranger. As soon as she saw him, she broke away and ran to him, throwing her arms around him.

"This might be the wrong time," he said. "But I'm glad you're selling the house."

"And I'm going to take you up on your offer," she said. "But we're not shacking up. I'm paying rent and I want my own bedroom."

"Deal."

Whitehorse came over to them and shook Hank's hand. "Great to see y'all again. Of course, the circumstances aren't the best."

"How'd you fit Jakes into the back of the transport vehicle?" Hank asked.

"Oh, we squeezed him in there." Whitehorse's smile was thin and sharp. "Real tight. We've picked up all but one of his SWAT guys after we raided their hideout. And we recovered all of the material contents from the two coffins."

"It's a fortune," Agatha said.

Whitehorse laughed. "Actually, it's worthless."

"How so? We saw the third and fourth coffins. They were loaded," she said.

"What can I say? The Nun was brilliant. All the gold and diamonds found in the caskets were counterfeit, and I'm guessing she lived a long and happy life with her fortune. What we do have is very detailed ledgers of blackmail and deeds being forcibly signed over."

"How's that going to work?" Hank asked.

"Well, we'll contact the families legally entitled to the property and mineral rights then we'll start the process of getting things set to rights. It's not out of the realm of possibility that the original owners might still be alive, but especially their direct descendants."

"You mean the families will get their property back? All of their property?" Agatha asked.

"Yep," Whitehorse beamed with pride. The families of Margaret Scott, Penelope Pennywell, Ruth Anne Wilkerson and Emma Gurtz have benefited from the proceeds of ill-gotten gains for long enough. It was illegally acquired. The law still stands, even after all these years."

"What about the Nun, or as we've heard, Sister Rosa Anita Immaculate? Was she even a nun?" Hank asked.

"We've checked with the Franciscan community of Poor Clare Nuns of Perpetual Adoration in San Antonio, but their official position is one of silence."

"No kidding," Hank chuckled.

"But, while we have the services of the good Dr. Andrew Lawrence in our midst, I think we can persuade him to track down the truth about her."

Epilogue

SATURDAY

Hank had turned off the alarm on his cell the night before. He'd needed the rest, but he was up early anyway. He grabbed his breakfast banana and a can of Ensure and headed out back to the patio. It was chilly outside, but he'd wrapped up in his robe and slippers. He turned on the fireplace outside and then sat back to enjoy his breakfast.

"So, let's see what's happening back in Philly," he muttered to himself as he flipped on the iPad and began to read the news.

It had been a very hectic week, and he was thankful for the solitude. That was a luxury he never had while running after serial killers with the FBI. Matter of fact, there was rarely a time when he could recall having complete peace in his life. There was always some drama going down that he'd have to deal with. It was nice out back, and all he wanted to do was enjoy the quiet.

He heard his back gate open and watched Coil come around the side of the house.

"Hey, stranger," Hank said, raising his brows.

"A guy pulls a gun on you, it makes you question whether or not you're welcome."

Hank rolled his eyes. "Don't be so dramatic. You deserved it. I probably wouldn't have shot you. You know you're always welcome."

Coil took the seat across from him and warmed his hands in front of the fire.

"I don't think Dot Williams is going to cause much more trouble for anyone," he said.

"Seems like Whitehorse discovered in their deed search that Dot's grandfather was a frequent visitor to The Church. He was a judge, and ripe for the blackmailing, especially since he managed to get not one, but two, of the serving girls who worked at The Church pregnant."

"Good old Judge Williams," Hank said.

"The trick is in order for Dot to have a legal right to the property, she must sign an affidavit acknowledging that she's the heir, and that she understands Wilber Williams was engaged in immoral and illicit behavior and waives all rights to sue or hold the state of Texas responsible for changes, damages, or modifications to the property being returned to the estate of Wilber Williams."

"No way," Hank said with a gasp.

"Yep, and get this," Coil said. "If the mothers of the babies he sired can be identified, they can make a claim to the estate. The best part is the property is way out in west Texas. Looks like Dot is going to relocate to claim her fortune."

"Did I hear Dot Williams's name?" Agatha said, coming through the same gate Coil had entered earlier. "It's too early to be so negative." She was in her running gear, and she took the chair between Coil and Hank.

"Your archenemy will be leaving town soon," Coil told

her. "Hank can fill you in." He stood and put his cowboy hat on. "I've got to get into the office."

"So," Hank said. "What's on the agenda for today?"

"How do you feel about packing?"

"Are we going on a trip?" he asked.

"Well, I am," she said. "Just got the news that an offer was made on the house. I'm going to accept it. I figure it shouldn't take us too long to pack up and transport everything across the street. Right?"

"Hmm," Hank said. "I've got a better idea. Why don't I call a moving company, and they can take care of everything? You go throw a bathing suit and a couple changes of clothes into a bag, and we'll escape the madness somewhere warm and sunny."

She grinned. "I was hoping you'd say that."

Grime & Punishment - Story Highlight

Only politics are more crooked than crime. When it's election time in Bell County, Texas, the highly-coveted position of the jurisdiction's top cop brings opponents out swinging. The elected Sheriff is on the ballot after Reggie Coil was first voted in by a narrow margin four years earlier.

Coil has become a citizen favorite, but the people used to getting away with their own vices don't appreciate his honest and equal approach toward enforcing the law. A concerted effort to defeat the experienced lawman, plans to use his own past against him.

While still on an ethics violation probation that resulted from a tough decision made as a young undercover agent, Coil continues to walk on eggshells as the election approaches. His opposition delights in smashing the eggs, and Coil's career.

Hank Davidson is appointed as the interim Sheriff by Coil after he's been suspended pending the outcome of a bogus investigation. Hank's best resource for revealing the truth to set Coil free is Agatha Harley. They've created a life and love from solving crimes together, and as Hank draws closer to asking her to marry him, life in Rusty Gun seems to continually get in his way.

Two things Hank is sure of; he will propose to Agatha soon, and Reggie Coil is the best man for the job.

Liliana and I have loved sharing these stories in our Harley & Davidson Mystery Series with you.

There are many more adventures to be had for Aggie and Hank. Make sure you stay up to date with life in Rusty Gun, Texas by signing up for our emails.

Thanks again and please be sure to leave a review where you bought each story and, recommend the series to your friends.

Kindly,
Scott & Liliana

Enjoy this book? You can make a big difference

Reviews are so important in helping us get the word out about Harley and Davidson Mystery Series. If you've enjoyed this adventure Liliana & I would be so grateful if you would take a few minutes to leave a review (it can be as short as you like) on the book's buy page.

Thanks,
Scott & Liliana

Dirty Deeds

Dirty Laundry

Dirty Money

A Dirty Job

Addison Holmes Mystery Series

Whiskey Rebellion

Whiskey Sour

Whiskey For Breakfast

Whiskey, You're The Devil

Whiskey on the Rocks

Whiskey Tango Foxtrot

Whiskey and Gunpowder

Books by Liliana Hart and Scott Silverii

The Harley and Davidson Mystery Series

The Farmer's Slaughter

A Tisket a Casket

I Saw Mommy Killing Santa Claus

Get Your Murder Running

Deceased and Desist

Malice In Wonderland

Tequila Mockingbird

Gone With the Sin

The Gravediggers

The Darkest Corner

Gone to Dust

Say No More

Lawmen of Surrender (MacKenzies-1001 Dark Nights)

Also by Scott Silverii

Liliana Hart is a New York Times, USAToday, and Publisher's Weekly bestselling author of more than sixty titles. After starting her first novel her freshman year of college, she immediately became addicted to writing and knew she'd found what she was meant to do with her life. She has no idea why she majored in music.

Since publishing in June 2011, Liliana has sold more than six-million books. All three of her series have made multiple appearances on the New York Times list.

Liliana can almost always be found at her computer writing, hauling five kids to various activities, or spending time with her husband. She calls Texas home.

If you enjoyed reading *this*, I would appreciate it if you would help others enjoy this book, too.

Lend it. This e-book is lending-enabled, so please, share it with a friend.

Recommend it. Please help other readers find this book by recommending it to friends, readers' groups and discussion boards.

Review it. Please tell other readers why you liked this

book by reviewing. If you do write a review, please send me an email at lilianahartauthor@gmail.com, or visit me at http://www.lilianahart.com.

Connect with me online:
www.lilianahart.com
lilianahartauthor@gmail.com

facebook.com/LilianaHart

twitter.com/Liliana_Hart

instagram.com/LilianaHart

bookbub.com/authors/liliana-hart

Liliana's writing partner and husband, Scott Silverii blends over 25 years of heart-stopping policing Special Operations experience.

From deep in the heart of south Louisiana's Cajun Country, his action-packed writing style is seasoned by the Mardi Gras, hurricanes and crawfish étouffée.

Don't let the easy Creole smile fool you. The author served most of a highly decorated career in SOG buying dope, banging down doors, and busting bad guys.

Bringing characters to life based on those amazing experiences, Scott writes it like he lived it.

Lock and Load – Let's Roll.

CPSIA information can be obtained
at www.ICGtesting.com
Printed in the USA
LVHW091437100520
655302LV00008B/2556

9 781951 129040